Her days in Dubai

Mehraveh Firouz

Title: Her days in Dubai
ISBN: 9781739660338

Author:
Mehraveh Firouz
Illustrator:
Shirin Malekesmaili

Firouz Media Limited
www.firouzmedia.com
IG: @firouzmedia

Author's note:

With sincere gratitude, I feel blessed by having Gianna, Stacey, and Edi, for their time, support, and insight...

The story's idea came from Anaik. She usually took daily walks by the sea in Hastings, and was mesmerized by the authentic fishing industry of that town, and also its beautiful and daunting land-scape.

I started to develop a story out of it. Then a talented screenwriter, named Phil O'Sullivan took care of the working title which was *Green Beanie Girl,* and turned my story into a script. There were some talks to shoot that movie script but it didn't happen.

Years later, I had to travel to Dubai on several occasions. This was the time I understood the profound culture and history of the fishing industry in Dubai. Therefore, I decided to bring my main character, Iman, to Dubai instead of Hastings. It makes more sense now...

PROLOGUE

Iman gazed fixedly at the body in front of her. She was amazed that death could be so swift. She'd seen in countless movies; but the reality felt different.

Her knees dug into the sand. With her eyes wide open, the woman stared vacantly into the night sky, not seeing a thing. The unblinking stare made Iman rather curious. Now she was wondering – wondering what could have happened to this woman – wondering what it felt like to die. Was there something special about it?

She shifted her gaze to the place where the woman had been stabbed. Fresh drops of blood were still trickling from it. The place of penetration was dark red and covered with patches of fibrin. Around her neck were bruises and fingerprints, and her lips were chapped. What she hadn't learnt from horror movies was that right now, the dead woman was slowly going into rigor mortis.

Next she shifted her gaze slowly to the murder weapon lying just beside her. It was a small knife gleaming, camouflaged by the silvery moonlight overhead.
It had a red handle which seemed strange.
Don't they all seem strange? Iman asked herself. But if this little thing could take a whole life, then a chainsaw from her favorite movie could make short work of the flesh. She didn't get a chance to find out, because then her eyes

rose, alerted by a sound, and found those of the person who had wielded the blade moments ago. Right there, the girl felt her blood chill within her veins. She could have sworn, he saw her.

He saw her.

CHAPTER ONE

The chainsaw ground and grated – a blood-curdling scream, distinctively feminine. And then the sound of it tearing through flesh, and blood splattering everywhere – the scream instantly subsided into a dead faint. The camera focused on lifeless eyes quickly, a confirmation of the job of the chainsaw and its wielder.

Iman was sitting on a bench in the shades behind a boat across the harbor comfortably watching a horror movie with her iPad. It was midnight. The creek had gone quiet as the fishermen had retired for the night. But it was the perfect time for Iman to watch her horror movies, with no disturbance at all. Well, save the few sounds and ripples from within the creek.

She giggled as the man wielding the chainsaw in the movie revved it and headed for his next victim; the boyfriend of the previous one, it seemed.

The creek was not sufficiently illuminated, and so Iman was perfectly hidden in the dark, away from prying eyes. The small light from lanterns positioned around the creek was shared across the large expanse, and was blocked on different paths by fishing nets, *gargoors*, baskets of fish and crab boxes stacked high in one of the planes, and hand-lines piled on another plane. There were also tents in the creek – camps for the local fishermen just in case they did not finish their work for the day or hoped to start early in the morning.

Somewhere across the expanse of the creek was the fish market. There were also cooling vans and deep freezers around. The smell of fish saturated the atmosphere around this area. But having nowhere else to go, Iman found it comfortable here.

She continued to watch the movie on her iPad whilst chuckling, caring less about everything else around her. It was just her and the thrilling events that transpired in the movie. She waved her hand across the screen in pursuit of a moth that had just perched on it, attracted by the glow. The thing left just in time for a new jump-scare scene to be witnessed with full focus.

A foreign sound snapped that focus loose.

Iman had not noticed she had company and had only been alerted by the cough that escaped the lips of the man that now sat dangerously close to her. She stopped for a moment, alerted by the sound. That moment was all it lasted for. Her face quickly resumed a blank expression. She slowly looked up from the iPad screen, tucking some strands of hair that had escaped her beanie back in, to the shoes of the stranger. They were awfully in the shape of a boat, ironically. Her gaze didn't linger long enough to revel in its fascination. She proceeded to observe the tunic the man was clad in, up his turban and to the shawl around his head and neck. He had a stubble across his jaw and a handle-bar mustache.

After taking a moment to pause the movie and rid the night of the noise, she took note of the boat the stranger was sitting on. It was the type of canoe the fishermen made used of; an old thing that had seen better years but still wouldn't fall apart anytime soon. And, fairly, she blamed herself for not taking note of his presence sooner. This looked to be just a regular fisherman, but it could have been someone else. Someone more dangerous.

"Who are you, little girl?" the man asked, his accent drenched over the words like many of the natives around the creek.

The moonlight overhead cast a dark grey hue on the creek, and so Iman could not really make out the expression on his face. But the gruffly sound of his voice told her it was pretty steely. Iman was not moved, nonetheless. Her hand simply clutched her iPad tighter, as if to say, "You're not taking it away from me."

Deciding the fisherman would be in more use of actual words, she allowed her lips offer something. "My name is Iman," she answered softly.

The man looked at her keenly as if to get a better view of this little girl sitting alone in the dark and watching a movie only the brave watched in the middle of the night. He had obviously been alerted by the sound of all the screaming and the horrors, but he seemed to carefully ignore it. And then he asked, a mix of emotions in his voice, "What are you doing here?"

Iman didn't have an answer to that and so kept quiet, looking down at the broken iPad screen and rubbing it gently. If people didn't receive answers to their questions, they tended to conjure a stretch of likely possibilities and settle on the worst or the best. Iman had had enough experience with these fishermen to know that. This man was no exception. She could almost imagine the muscles around his eyes softening and his lips pressing together grimly.

"Does your father own a barn here, or maybe work here?" he asked as his tone adjusted to a more concerned one. He looked around curiously, almost as though in expectation for an adult to rise out of the darkness − or the waters − to claim her. They both knew that wasn't going to happen.

Iman kept mute, still head bent. The man heaved a sigh. He seemed to have exhausted his questions.

"It's late," he said finally. "You should bring down the volume of that movie. We could literally hear it from a distance. Or better still, you put the phone away and sleep. That doesn't seem like something a kid should be watching so late." His distaste at the choice of movie wasn't hard to take note of.

Iman remained silent. If not of the words she'd said earlier, she was sure the man would have thought she was mute. The man gazed at her briefly, made a movement to add something else but stopped himself, and then padded away. Iman looked up at him for a while as he went away, looking back at intervals. He didn't seem to need a light to move across the water. The general direction of his destination was a cluster of tents lit with lanterns at one end of the creek.

This was not a good sign for the night. She had always tried to stay off the prying eyes of people in this creek, and for so long already. These were the questions she was avoiding. This night, she had stayed far away from the center of the creek. How come this man could hear the sound from the movie she was watching? And how could she bring down the volume of the iPad? The sound was the fun. It was the life of the movie. But she soon concluded it was best she moved away from there.

Words would spread, like it usually did amongst fishermen on hot afternoons, and people might be on the look out for her. That wasn't a chance she was willing to entertain.

Then, as if in an urge to get her moving away, the sky rumbled. Across the sea was a tempest raging. The wind howled pitilessly as Iman ran across the harbor. Iman looked around and found an abandoned canal boat somewhere. Well, it looked abandoned, and didn't seem like it would float if placed on water. It was perfect. She trudged towards it – the wind blew harshly against her face. She was shivering now despite the coat she had wrapped around her body.

She got to the boat – a pretty large one. With her iPad tucked carefully within her coat. She leaped up and grabbed the rim of the fuselage. She gathered momentum and hauled herself onto the boat. Her steps were light, lest the thing crumbled upon her weight. She promptly realized it could hold her well enough.

Quickly, she pushed at the door, but it was jammed shut. With as much strength as she could gather, she pulled again and again – but the door wouldn't budge. Iman found herself glancing around, wondering if she'd been unfortunate enough to garner any attention, given the sound of her struggle.

No.

She carefully looked at the left side of the cabin and found a broken window. Then she momentarily checked to see if there was anything to be cautious of within. She'd seen enough of those horror movies to ensure her vigilance (which had been put to shame just minutes ago) and care.

"Okay," she muttered to herself upon confirming the abandoned boat was empty. Making sure not to cause more damage to her iPad, or a shard of glass jutting out the window slice through her flesh, she eased her way through.

It was old and rusty in here. The floorboards creaked beneath her feet as she sat on the floor, leaning her back against the wall. Her breath formed a trail in the cold. She zipped down her coat and took out her iPad and then zipped it back up. The cabin had low acoustics and so it deadened the sound of the movie as she watched on.

All the murder and blood were her only comfort as the night went on, and the sky eventually set loose the rain. She wasn't ready for what would come if she drifted to sleep. But no manner of gore and horror kept Iman from falling asleep. Eventually, she did, and it happened.

CHAPTER TWO

Iman did not dream of a masked man with a chainsaw or a group of bodies with dismembered limbs. No, her mind conjured up something different. She dreamt of a woman; a tall woman with silky dark hair, a chin drawn with severe strokes and the most beautiful brown eyes. The woman smelt like sweets and pastries and she had sugar upon her hair. The green beanie she usually used, in place of a chef's hat, to shield her hair from the specks of sugar had been passed down to someone else. Someone who now watched the woman gingerly.

The woman did not mind. She hummed carefully as she whisked her batter with a grace worthy of angels, swirling around the kitchen without any care in the world. Iman was there too, beanie upon her head though they were indoors. Her mind seemed to process the tiniest details of the kitchen. The pristine tiles, the modern utensils, the baked goods upon the counter, and the very welcoming smell of it all. She found herself holding on to all those feelings as if it was the last time it would happen, and she wished she could remain in this loop forever.

It didn't matter. Her grip upon the moment slipped. There was a cut in-between moments, Iman noticed, because the woman was now standing beside her and the batter was out of sight, her knees bent and her full lips spread in a broad smile.

"It'll be ready soon and you'll be very happy," she said, muting

her humming. There was a sting on Iman's finger, barely noticeable but the woman kissed the finger as though that action would heal the dressed wound. She adjusted the beanie upon Iman's head and smiled again. Right then, the vision blurred further. Iman realized she didn't recognize the woman anymore. She remembered bits and pieces… silky dark hair… brown eyes… soothing voice… beautiful--

The knock on the door was the first sign that something bad was about to happen. The both of them snapped their attention towards the living room. Iman wanted to reach out and tell the woman not to answer the door. Focus on the beanie she was adjusting. She wanted to take back the moment to the singing and the baking. Maybe she did, for the slightest instant. It fractured quickly and the woman was now shifting away from Iman, reaching for a scarf to wrap her hair as the knock continued. Her graceful movements towards the door didn't stop despite Iman's desperate attempts to stop it.

There was another cut in-between moments because the door was already open now, bringing in the glimmer of the hot afternoon sun into the house, and a man in a black suit. He was blurry too. White skinned… controlled and monotone voice… polished black shoes… blue eyes. No, green. They were green. None of those pieces formed into anything concrete. It was more of an idea than an actual person. They spoke in muted whispers. There was an argument. A struggle? Didn't really seem like it. Arguments required two parties speaking violently but only one of them seemed to be doing that.

Cut!

The woman was on the floor, crying, and the suited man was trying to help her up with little success. Iman felt her limbs move forward. Her heartbeat rose and she felt an expansion in her chest… it didn't feel good. A strange feeling washed over her bronze skin, causing some bumps to rise. This shouldn't be happening. Despite her mind's best attempts to turn back the moment to the happier times when she was smiling, it always came back to this moment.

Broken words reached her ears. "Husband... Killed... Dead." Iman couldn't breathe. There was something causing the stress upon her lungs and she soon started coughing. The three of them realized it too late.

Cookies. Oven. Smoke. Repeat.

Iman felt her mind begin to get weighed down from everything. Nothing made sense anymore. It all came into her mind in disjointed pieces of a puzzle, and the swelling in her chest didn't stop. Her vision blurred and everything began to spin aimlessly. There was only one constant in every piece and flash. The woman. Then she screamed.

"Mum!"

It wasn't a dream. It was a memory.

***

By the time Iman woke up the next morning, the creek was already buzzing with life. The fishermen had begun to let their canoes into the water and cast their nets while chatting loudly. There were customers at the market already despite the fact that the sun had barely poked its head out of the clouds. Luckily, Iman had not been awoken by anyone but the whirring sounds of the boats and other fishing equipment, and of course, the hustle and bustle of the fishing market. Perhaps the incident from the other night would not come back to bite her.

She slouched up from the corner of the boat she'd huddled in and stretched like a hard rubber – her skin nearly snapped. She yawned deeply and adjusted her dress which she had worn for two days now since she managed a bath in the smelly waters. The dress had clearly seen better days and she needed to get herself into clean clothes.

Lazily moving forward, Iman came by the edge of the broken window and breathed in the fishy smell of the morning, synced with an oddly comforting smell from last night's rain. She looked across the harbor and the small town that had cross-faded into it. There was a hotel of sorts being built at one side, taking up an expanse of space. The engineers were at work already. Words around the harbor was that the owner of the hotel had put a lot of stolen money into the building. Iman barely focused on it. Flies buzzed around – the stench in the creek could make a person puke their guts out if they weren't used to it already.

With sleek movements, Iman helped herself out of the boat she had made her home, careful not to be seen by anyone. Iman rubbed on her eyes and trudged across the sands towards the denser part of the area. She had drained her iPad the previous night and needed to find a place to charge it.

It was easy to dissolve into the chaos of the street. Iman liked to think of the whole area as a work of art. The way the town blended with the fishing settlement and the harbor was nothing short of an artist's work. It was even hard to tell where the town began. It was like being lured into an entirely different world. The buildings themselves were works of arts themselves. The geometric residences lined the side of the street in a straight line. That did not prevent vendors from finding places to set up their little shops. There was a burst of colorful tents and goods to be sold along the street, like a parade leading up to the fish market where the actual chaos was nestled.

As she walked past people along the street, now away from the creek, they held their noses. She reeked of raw fish and like someone who hadn't had a bath in days. What was to be expected anyway? The people gawked at her and sniffed. Iman paid not the tiniest attention to it. She took purposeful steps despite not knowing where exactly she was headed. But perhaps if she had thought about the reactions around her, she wouldn't have noticed the woman she just saw. Iman felt a flutter within her. The woman had black hair and wide eyes… they were all too familiar. Despite the situation around her, Iman could have sworn she perceived sweets and sugar in the air. Her feet melted.

The woman was heading towards the fish market, it appeared. Her form was wrapped within a black dress and she held a basket in hand, easing her way through the chaos of the street.

"Yes, that must be her," Iman heard her mind say. For the first time in days, she felt something that was dangerously like hope.

Iman followed the woman behind, but kept her presence unnoticed. She had to first confirm her suspicions before going up to her, lest she scared the woman. The woman did not notice for once that she was being trailed. Iman hid behind lamp posts, post boxes, and other objects along the road anytime she noticed that the woman was about to look back. All of this was much to the distaste of the people who were near wherever she took cover, of course. One man even went as far as spitting near Iman and cussing at her in Arabic. She knew it was a cuss because she'd heard it far too many times. That hadn't been enough to break Iman's focus.

Eventually, the woman herself seemed to have noticed that someone was keeping tracks of her. Any sane person would. Iman prided herself in her vigilance and care, but not in her stealth or ability to trail a person. The woman did not stop looking back and walking faster, past shops and through a wave of people. And the foul smell that preceded Iman seemed to give her presence away. No kidding about that. The smell could have woken dead fishes.

The woman finally arrived at the fish market, which was more chaotic than the streets. Iman watched from behind a stack of baskets as she made her transactions. The woman's alert was almost entirely gone. She had probably thought Iman was a thief or something who had eventually gotten bored. She didn't find Iman where she hid and watched.

Something told Iman to step forward and finally make a confirmation about who the person was. This could put an end to her search. No more sleeping in abandoned boats and stolen tents. No more going hungry either, and it would certainly mean cleaner and less smelly clothes. Iman allowed herself give into that fantasy. That was her mistake, because right then, Iman heard the woman speaking Arabic. That was not a language the one she searched for could speak, and that voice… it wasn't her. She lost interest and immediately went back into the streets, wandering from one end to another and dissolving into the chaos.

It was after she had followed another woman to a grocery and noticed that she also spoke Arabic that she gave up. She was hungry. One could hardly blame her since it was almost noon and she hadn't had anything to eat. The stolen bread from yesterday evening couldn't take her forever anyway.

Now walking slowly, with her iPad clutched in her hand, she went into a nearby restaurant. Behind the counter was a man who could have either been in his early forties or late thirties. He wore a striped apron with its sleeves rolled around the elbow. He had a full beard across his jaw, anointed with a handful of greying ones. He had been attentive on the report shown on the TV hung across a part of the wall. His attention was, however, arrested by the jiggling of the door as Iman walked in.

She was standing by the door, looking around as though she had no idea where she was.

"What can I do for you, miss?" the man asked.

Iman brought her eyes slowly at him. "Do you have an outlet where I can charge my iPad, please?" she requested.

CHAPTER THREE

Erol Bilginer was not supposed to be here. At least, that was what he'd been telling himself for several months. He pushed himself up to his feet and observed his reflection in the mirror. If his mother were here, she would have nagged him until he'd shaved all his beards. But since she wasn't, he slid away from the mirror and moved towards the door of his apartment. He lived in a fairly big building. It was one of the ones that had been standing for many generations here in Deira. Many memories and lives had been forged within its old and beautiful walls. And now, Erol's was being forged. He hated it. The building was joined with a restaurant at the front. A restaurant which many of his family members had ran for years, and which had now been passed down to him upon his mother's death.

He straightened and swore as he came into the dimly-lit restaurant. He unlocked the door and came outside to the ridiculously bright morning. Groaning, Erol strolled towards the meat truck that had awoken him minutes ago with its horn.

"Ah, Erol, still sleeping, I see?" a young man said, leaning against the truck with a box in hand. Ahmed. His skin was paler compared to Erol, probably because he spent all his time hardening his heart in a freezer. They both had dark eyes, but where Ahmed's was thinner and slanted, Erol's were like circular things with darkened surroundings.

Erol grunted. "I kept the shop open really late last night, hoping more people will come back," he said bitterly as the sleep began to finally shrug off his demeanor.

The meat seller obviously didn't care enough about that. Ahmed definitely had better things to worry about. All that mattered to him now was his weekly sale to Erol's restaurant and the money he made. Still, he shook his head, out of controlled politeness, and said, "Don't worry. Things will get better." His focus had shifted to the money Erol handed him and was now counting it. Erol shrugged.

"Maybe it would if you didn't make only *kebabs*," a new voice said. The two men turned towards the older woman coming towards them with a cane.

"*Ahlan wa sahlan*, Fatima," they both said to her, bowing just the slightest. The meat seller proceeded to give Erol a look that seemed to say, "Good luck," before he ran quickly to the driver's seat of his truck.

Fatima kept dragging herself forward, momentarily offering a reply to their greetings by saying, "*Ahlan biki*." Fatima looked like she was old enough to be Erol's mother. She was quite short and fat, with greying hair that had been wrapped up in her scarf. Her cane was to help the limp from a wound she probably suffered while gossiping. Her timing couldn't have been worse.

Erol grunted something behind his shoulder and made for his building.

"Wait, Erol," called Fatima, helplessly. " My roof is leaking. Who could guess these rainy days in Dubai? The rain last night came pouring on my cat's head." There was a plea in her voice.

A hint of a smile settled on Erol's face and it was a miracle it didn't extend into a snort. The woman's cats could get wet for all he cared for. Still, he paused, clutching his carton of meat tightly like it was a child. It was perfectly frozen and quite heavy too. This wasn't the time for chitchatting. "I have told you, Fatima, I am not a carpenter or a plumber or an electrician. Stop calling me every time you have the slightest problem. You should get people to fix your stuff. Don't always come to me." He offered a smile for good measures before turning around, hoping his reply would be enough to send her back across the street to the house she shared with possibly a hundred cats.

Of course, Fatima wasn't satisfied with that reply.

"This is why you don't have a wife," she said sharply and accusingly. True enough, Erol turned around to see her cane lifted in the air towards his face. "You just stay around making kebabs and grumbling like someone stole from you. You have a *djinn* in you and you should pray." Her tone was sharp and she said every word as though it was the end of the sentence, causing an unnecessary stress in her voice.

"People love kebab," Erol told her, scoffing. He realized his tone had gone defensive but didn't mind. One could complain about his status as a bachelor or his behavior, but not the food his family had been making at the end of this street all his life. He pushed the cane away from his face and felt his nose flare. "My family has been making kebabs in these parts for a very long time and everyone loves us." He knew that was a lie. If it wasn't, he would have been getting a lot of customers. At this rate, he feared the restaurant would close down. Perhaps it was about time he returned to his real estate management job. That way, he would be far away from Fatima, at least.

Fatima snorted even as Erol approached the door of his restaurant. "Everybody here likes fish. Fish! If you eat meat, you get fat and die," she told him. A part of Erol wondered why that hadn't happened to Fatima yet.

"Fatima, if I agree to fix your roof, will you leave me alone?" Erol found himself whispering dejectedly. The woman was a walking natural disaster. It was a mystery how she managed to still be alive.

His words seemed to allow what looked like a smile rise upon her lips though. It was a very terrible smile. "Yes. You should also get a wife. Zeenat's daughter just came back from London and--"

"Okay, I will think about it too," yelled Erol. Anything to make her quit bugging him on this already annoying morning. Using his feet, he pushed the wooden door of his restaurant open and was all too willing to slam it in Fatima's face when she placed her cane in front of it and peered at him through the small opening.

Fatima's eyes looked around before leaning closer to him. There was seriousness within those eyes now coupled with something that looked like fear, and maybe that was what made Erol relax to hear what she had to say this time.

"I heard the fishermen talking about a spirit girl by the harbor. They said she stands at the edge, screaming and making sounds like a blender. You should be careful," she whispered dangerously. There was genuine concern in her words though.

Erol didn't know why he expected her to have anything useful to say. He simply offered her a tight smile and nodded. Fatima was always superstitious, talking about djinn and ghosts and other impossible things she had allegedly seen in the area. "I will be on the lookout, Fatima," Erol told her kindly, hoping that would be enough to send her away from his doorstep. He didn't want her scaring away the handful of customers he usually got in the first place.

"And you should pray more oft--"

Now, Erol slammed the door shut, shutting her up. Fatima cussed loudly in Arabic before moving away. Erol heaved a sigh as he turned around and made his way to the freezer behind the counter of his shop where he dropped the meat. He rolled up his sleeves, wore his apron, and switched on the TV. The news that was being broadcast was from the popular Creek Observer. There was a woman interviewing some fishermen about the living conditions in the Creek.

There didn't seem to be any mention of the spirit girl Fatima had been terrified of.

Smiling to himself, Erol proceeded to get the restaurant straightened up, open the windows, and make his way back to the other end of the counter where he waited for his first customer to come prancing through the double doors, all the while entertaining himself with the television.

Erol had only began to relax behind the counter when the bell rang and a figure eased her way though. For a moment, maybe thanks to Fatima, he expected a spirit or a djinn to come in. But it was just a little girl, and she had asked him the oddest question.

"Do you have an outlet where I can charge my iPad, please?"

The girl couldn't have been over twelve. Probably younger. Her appearance wasn't like what Erol was used to see upon Deira's street. Her skin was a pure bronze that held a beautiful, though dirty, face. Her eyelashes were long and they fluttered as she blinked. She wasn't that close to Erol but he could easily pick out the alluring shade of brown that was her eyes. It was as though someone had picked up a jar of honey and poured it in her eyes.

Her beauty did not extend to her appearance. Her small form was wrapped within a big black coat. She had a green beanie on her head too, and she brought quite a stench with her. He wondered if she'd lost her way or something and did not truly intend to come here. Erol hated to admit but this but the girl could as well be a spirit.

He refused to let Fatima get to him this morning. So he cocked a brow and adjusted his weight behind the counter. "You can check the wall socket on your left," he replied, finally, pointing towards the socket.

The girl looked to her side and found the socket. She walked slowly to it and plugged in her iPad which she pulled out from within her huge coat. Erol watched her all while. He noticed how slow she walked and responded to actions. He was quite cautious. What else could be within that coat of hers?

"Thank you. Can I stay here and wait for it to charge full?" the girl asked, looking up at him meekly and allowing her eyelashes flutter. Her accent was strange. She certainly wasn't from around here. There was no kidding with that.

"It's all right. You can leave anytime you want," he agreed, his voice sounding tired. "Just… take a seat over there."

The girl seemed pleased with that. She looked like how Erol always felt after a tiring day at the restaurant, maybe even worse. She sat on the chair beside the counter, bringing along the smell with her. Erol controlled his retch and stopped himself from recoiling. He still didn't like the smell of the fish one bit. The girl didn't seem to realize the severity of her stench as she sank into the seat and lifted her head up, watching the program shown on the TV. Erol had switched it from Creek Observer to a channel that showed a Bollywood film. There was a lot of dancing which seemed to quickly bore the young girl. And so she only flicked glances at the TV from time to time.

Eventually, Erol found it wise to get the standing fan working, which did a whole lot in making the whole thing bearable. A part of him thought to turn the girl away or question her further about who she was and where she was from, and maybe she was the spirit girl Fatima mentioned. He didn't.

Half an hour went by, and the young girl was still waiting for her object of companionship to charge full. It was both embarrassing and annoying that not a single customer came into the shop. Erol found himself glancing at the time from time to time and lazily watching TV. He too had grown bored at some point and began tapping away on his phone while silently praying some customer would come around. He tried to convince himself it was the time of the day. Most people preferred their kebab at night.

Suddenly a sound drew his attention. He took a look from the counter at the strange girl who hung her head low. Her stomach began churning and growling again as if to assure Erol it had been responsible for the earlier noise. It wasn't hard to tell she was famished. The girl herself clutched her stomach and placed her gaze upon everything but Erol, perhaps hoping he hadn't heard that. There was no way anybody could have missed the sharp winces within the shores of her face, least of all the sound her stomach kept making.

"You look hungry. Do you mind if get you something to eat?" he offered. To be fair, he needed to serve someone. If he didn't, he could as well loose his sanity from the ridiculous absence of a customer. Looking at all the empty wooden chair and vacant tables really didn't sit well with him.

The girl looked up at him expectantly, like a puppy waiting for a treat from its owner, but there was an edge to her expression. Caution, maybe. He was a stranger after all.

"Look, you don't have to be afraid, all right?" Erol tried, momentarily itching his beard. He wasn't going to ignore a hungry child, neither would he do anything to harm her. Still, he couldn't miss the edge in her demeanor. Then he straightened, wore a small smile and continued, "My name is Erol. Erol Bilginer. And I own this place. I only noticed that you were--"

"No, I don't mind, sir," the young girl cut in.

Erol recoiled and swallowed back his words. He'd been wrong. That wasn't caution or fear in the girl's eyes. Those brown eyes were desperate. Now he understood how hungry she was. He was a little bit fascinated by her now. The way she sat and the way she spoke was refined, formal… almost like the way one would expect a princess to.

Nevertheless, he still wore a grin on his face to convince her he meant no harm as he shredded some kebab meat from the spit. He enjoyed the process. It was better than sitting around all day and waiting for customers that probably weren't going to come.

"The grill's only been on about an hour, but it should be nice and warm," he explained contentedly. The smell from his kebab totally pushed back the remnants of the stench the strange girl her brought in with her. Finally, Erol wrapped it in a pita with some salad, awfully pleased with himself. "Spicy?" he inquired.

With the same refined grace he'd noticed, she shook her head and swallowed hard as the aroma from the meat wafted through her nostrils. Erol chuckled and handed her the kebab. "Here," he said to her.

The girl stretched forward and took it from him. "Thank you," she said. The smile that fell into place on her face made his cold heart warm.

"You're welcome," Erol replied with a wide smile. Perhaps the first smile of his that hadn't been quite forced in a while.

There was a chime in the air and they both looked towards the corner. It appeared the girl's iPad had charged full at this time. She went and unplugged it. She reached for the door, but then she stopped. With her head bent, she turned back – Erol was watching her all the while. The glum look on his face was that of concern.

"Can you please give me food whenever I come here?" she asked.

Erol's face went pale with surprise. The space between his brows creased. He had not expected that. But how bold she was to make such request, he thought. "But I have only given you some food as it is my tradition for my first customer for the day. Believe me, miss, I…"

"My name is Iman," she told him.

"Oh…" he let out.

Erol nodded from left to right, wrinkling the corners of his mouth like one trying to get a first taste of chocolate. The girl, Iman, kept her penetrating gaze at him, giving him no choice to turn her down. At least, that was what it felt like she was doing. Those gleaming eyes of hers held incomprehensible emotions within their shores.

"It's pretty difficult… Iman," he insisted, straightening. In his head, he was already pulling together a string of words that he would serve her so she would understand how unprofitable it would be just offer her food every time. It wasn't even like he made enough money here in the first place. However, he didn't get a chance to say those words.

"But you are my friend, right?" Iman questioned. She

held his gaze.

Erol parted his lips, closed them and parted them again to speak. "Uh… yes, I guess. A bit of a stretch though considering I've known you for just a little over an hour. But this shop is the only thing I've got. Trust me, I want to help you, kid, but there's a lot involved here," he explained. He was getting pretty tired of the conversation already. This little thing was as persistent, and a bit annoying, as Fatima was. Not his favorite kinds of people.

"Please."

Erol exhaled deeply – he had finally surrendered. Maybe because he was used to finding the shorted route out of a situation that made him uncomfortable He looked down at the kebab Iman was holding in her hands. His brain drew up calculations, thinking how he could part with that every day. The cost wasn't some small thing. He tapped his fingers tentatively on the counter and glanced at the TV.

"All right. But it would be morning not night, okay?" he told her finally.
"Okay. Thank you," Iman said and left the shop.

Erol kept his eyes at her as she disappeared down the street. He kept wondering if he had made the right decision or not. His weakness had been the confidence Iman showed while making the request. It was as if she was certain he was going to agree no matter what. And eventually, he did.

Maybe this was the spirit girl Fatima spoke of indeed. Then in that case, Erol could say he'd simply been bewitched. His mortal mind couldn't resist the calls of the djinn. Maybe. Or maybe he thought of Iman arriving at her abode (be it the harbor or a house somewhere) at twilight. Maybe she would settle herself on a bench some distance away from people, open the kebab and with ravenous appetite and began to eat every piece amidst the pestering flies and smell around the creek. And just that thought alone, adding something useful in someone's life, made him quite proud of himself. That was why he did it, and he knew his mother would have rolled in his grave if he hadn't.

Holding that thought, Erol turned off his TV and left the restaurant, walking across the street to the first house he saw at the edge of the street. He knocked on the door and smile tightly at the woman who answered.

"Which part of your roof is leaking, Fatima?" he grumbled.

And he did that. None of them knew that in a few days from now, there would be a dead woman somewhere, and the killer now stood among them.

CHAPTER FOUR

For once, it seemed like luck had finally smiled on Iman. Hitherto, she had continued in her daily routine of trailing different women, but there had been no luck. None of them had been the one she'd been looking for, not to mention the stress of walking around the entire settlement on little to no food. Iman had made sure to have her bath though, eventually. She still made her way over to *Bilginer's Spicy Kebab* though, and true to his promise, Erol had given her breakfast every morning. Though at one point, a fat, old woman had given Iman an earful on how all that meat wasn't good for her body. She said something about getting a husband.

Erol had asked Iman where she was from or if she was lost. She knew he was simply giving into the urge to ask the questions he'd wanted to ask since they first met. But Iman had given no answer to those questions. She had been silent just as she was to the man at the creek the other day. The less they knew, the better. Moreover, Erol, like everyone else, had probably thought up the worst and best versions of what could have happened to her. He probably thought she was a child that might have been through a lot, and was looking forward to the day he would loosen her tongue. Everyone liked a good mystery.

Iman didn't think it would happen soon. It would be nice if someone could bind that old woman's tongue though.

This night, Iman had wandered into a clothing shop. Soft music graced the air, and it wasn't hard to notice the shop attendant keeping an eye on Iman. Iman didn't really care. She loved the way the shop felt. It was just like the town; a work of art. There was a burst of colors and various types of patterns upon fabrics. Iman wound her way around it, feeling the texture of every piece of fabric she could lay her hand on. It was as if she had come to buy some, but her reason for being here was pretty obvious. Well, to her, not to the attendant who had an awfully big nose.

As Iman silently navigated from section to section of the clothing shop, her eyes inadvertently caught a woman. She was making selections of some lingerie down the shop. Iman quickly dissolved behind a stack of clothes.

She steadied her breath and looked again. The woman was still checking out the lingerie. Iman couldn't help but follow her immediately, while using the clothes as cover. There was an attraction Iman couldn't resist – a resemblance of some sort. The woman had a lean frame, with big wide eyes, warm complexed and a raven-black hair that shoved out of the hoodie she wore. This could be the woman she had been looking for.

Iman followed her around the clothing shop, making sure she did not lose sight of her. And from behind a rail of clothes, she watched as the woman went into the changing room. She was convinced this was the woman she had been looking for. And even though she had found her at night, she would tail her movement – besides, the dark was the perfect cover.

Shortly after, the woman emerged from the room, carrying a bag and wearing a pleased expression upon her face. Iman waited until she exited the door of the clothing shop. She had spent just a little time with the big-nosed attendant before that finally happened.

Just as Iman was about to also make her way out of the shop, she felt a force grab hold of her arm. "Got you, little thief," snarled the big-nosed attendant who was not standing in front of the counter. She had a snarky grin and peered down on Iman like she was nothing but a rat. Her accent was nothing like what was heard on the streets of Deira. She sounded… British. "What have you been doing snooping around my shop? You think you can just steal form me and run away?"

Iman looked to the window where the form of the woman was beginning to disappear. Her head heaved anxiously. Her attention soon returned to the woman who still held a firm grip on her. "I did not steal anything," she said, a bit of plea in her voice while her eyes blazed spitefully at the woman's accusation.

"We'll see about that." The woman dragged Iman closer to the counter and said, "Take off that ridiculous coat of yours." Iman nodded. However, the moment the woman left her wrist, Iman pounced towards the door like a jungle cat. She burst into the night street of Deira, narrowly missing a motorcycle that was coming her way.

By the time she came out of the shop, the woman was nowhere in sight. Iman looked around the busy street with wide eyes. Her attention snapped when she heard the door of the clothing store come open and saw the attendant standing in front of the door.

"Somebody stop that thief," yelled the woman. Iman visibly shrugged. What was the woman's problem? She hadn't taken anything. Maybe she would have proceeded to go explain to the woman all of that but right then, her gaze found a hooded woman. The woman had rounded towards a lonelier street, unaware of anything. It seemed she was busy on her phone. Iman didn't let go of her sight this time. She followed her, dashing into the street and towards the corner the woman had taken.

Maybe it was luck or something, the store attendant hadn't been too keen to burst into the street like Iman had had. And no one seemed to have heard her calling Iman a thief. If they had then they clearly didn't care about it. With that advantage, Iman made sure she'd quickly disappeared into the shadowed part of the town she had seen the hooded woman going.

The woman had not the slightest idea that she was being followed. Her strides weren't fast and she lazily clung to the bag of clothes she'd bought while gluing her focus on her phone. She laughed momentarily at something she was watching, and that was as much as Iman heard from her before they resumed in silence. Iman maintained complete stealth. It was easier this time unlike the other times she'd been trailing women all over town. The dark helped, her hunger didn't. Eventually, the woman arrived at a building and entered. This wasn't a part of town Iman had ever found herself. One would think that with all the time she spent trailing woman, she would have covered every inch of the town. But this place was different. It held a certain chill and wrapped all the buildings with it tenderly. The houses here held the same geometric beauty Iman was already used to. But it was lonely. If she listened carefully, she could hear sounds within, but there was still a certain absence of life. And this very building the woman lazily eased herself into was the most lifeless of them all. The building itself looked like it had seen better days, at least, from what the full moon could provide.

Iman was by the road, thinking if it was wise to follow her or not. But then suddenly she noticed an upstairs light flick on. She could see the woman's shadow – it appeared as if she was undressing and changing into something else. Iman surmised that she could be going out again. Hopefully. If that wasn't the case, she would have to finally confront her and confirm if she was the one Iman had been searching desperately for. And so she waited outside patiently. With her beanie giving her face the perfect shade in the moonlight, she was pretty much undercover.

After a while, Iman noticed the light in the room go off, and then she heard the woman's heels knocking ceremoniously down the stairs. She ran and hid herself behind a palm tree nearby.

The woman finally touched the ground. She had changed into a furry coat on a skirt and a knee-high leather boots. She had a small bag swung across her shoulder. Looking at both sides of the road, she headed out – the sound of her heels knocking against the ground broke the silence of the night. That was a rather strange transition. Wherever the woman was headed, her night seemed like it was going to be eventful.

Even more curious than before, Iman followed the woman down a dark, isolated path. If Iman had thought the other place was lifeless, then she had no idea what to call this one. The area was surrounded by dilapidated construction trucks, fishing sheds and rusty boats – it was more like an unfinished warehouse, and closer to the sea too. Unlike the other area, this was a place Iman had found herself a few times. Iman looked around. A zephyr of the wind from the sea blew across her face, carrying that familiar smell.

Now the woman arrived at the path Iman was very much familiar with. There were crab boxes, fishing nets and baskets here and there. The woman stopped here – and so did Iman. She hid herself behind one of the pile of boxes in a *Gargoor*, waiting for whatever was about to happen.

From here, she saw the woman look around briefly and then rummaged in her bag and took out a stick of cigarette and a lighter. She flicked the lighter, but the flame was blown off by a gust of wind. She tried again and again, but the wind blew rather aimlessly. She flicked the lighter one last time and hooded the flame. The cigarette caught up like fronds and a wisp of smoke wriggled up in the air. It was obvious she was waiting for someone. Iman wanted to see it and did well not to make even the slightest of sound.

If she was being honest, the presence of the cigarette kinda put her off. The one she was searching for didn't smoke, to the best of her knowledge. But then, Iman's knowledge was very limited and quite blurry. She couldn't exactly trust whatever she thought she knew. Still, a part of her hoped this was the one and her search would be put to an end, maybe.

Under the moonlight, the woman's beauty was highlighted. In the absence of her hoodie, her dark hair ran down her back effortlessly like a piece of night cut form the sky and gleaming from the light of the moon. She noticed that the woman was losing her patience now. She was checking the time on her watch and looking up the sky. She drew in the cigarette and puffed grey clouds in the air which were blown away by the endless wind. She now sauntered about, murmuring to herself.

Suddenly, she seemed to remember something and delved in her bag, and then her pockets – Iman could tell she did not find what she was looking for.

"Shit!" she exclaimed she continued her little search, possibly hoping she'd simply been inadequate in finding it the first time.

And while she was still trying to remember where she had kept whatever it was she was looking for and puffing clouds of smoke in the air, a man padded out of nowhere and stood some distance away. Iman ducked a bit in response to the creepy way the man showed himself. She hated that she had, once again, not been vigilant enough to notice a boat coming until its presence was dangerously close-by. The canoe was like that of a fisherman's though. Iman frowned. He was obstructing her view now. He was tall and wore a cap that hid a greater part of his forehead. That was not a fisherman. Which made her wonder what he was doing with a boat like that.

The way he moved closer to the woman, who was still unaware of his presence, struck Iman as strange. If she didn't know better, she thought he was about to do something to her right then whilst her back was turned. And Iman wasn't sure if she, in fact, did know better.

CHAPTER FIVE

The crackling of the twig the man had just stepped on (accidentally, it seemed) as he walked closer to the woman startled her, causing her to jump and turn around.

"You're a fucking creep. You know that, right?" the woman huffed – her face had gone pale with the shock and she began to school the expression on her face as she recognized who it was.

She spoke the English language fluently but with an accent Iman couldn't quite fathom. Yet another proof this was not the one. Something made Iman hold on. Moreover, she couldn't really leave without alerting either of them. She hoped they would be done with their business soon though. As if on cue to her thoughts, the sky suddenly rumbled.

"My apologies. I didn't mean to frighten you," the man replied, looking up at the sky for a moment. His voice sounded cold and stern, just like that in Iman's movies. Still, there was a tint of eloquence to the way he spoke. His shoulders had fallen with her awareness of his presence, and he seemed to not be trying too hard to appear nonchalant. If Iman hadn't seen his earlier demeanor, she would have believed it like this woman currently appeared to.

"You're late," the woman told him flatly, seemingly not alerted by the way he spoke. She poured a cloud of smoke between them, maybe expecting another apology, but she got none. Iman couldn't see the man's face, but she could tell it was tight and had no friendly or informal gesture across it.

"I called, but…"

He was rather going to explain, but the woman cut in.

"Yeah, I left my phone… doesn't matter though."

She drew in another round of the cigarette as if her life depended on it and then poured the grey cloud of smoke up in the air – her lips assuming an O shape.

"So, I don't know what this weird fantasy is, but I'm not gonna screw you here. It smells like rotten fish around," she said, shuddering. It wasn't easy to tell if her shudder was from the cold or disgust. She took another look around, wearing the same measure of displeasure. Iman kept herself perfectly hidden in her lair.

The man shook his head. "That's not why I asked you to come. We need to talk," he said to her. Then his countenance just took a more direct expression. It was as displeased as the woman's but his was backed up with a stronger reason. Perhaps that was why the displeasure didn't fade as quickly as the woman's.

"The pub might've been a better choice then. I mean,

that's just me." The woman folded her arms, clinging gently to the cigarette and looked him squarely in the face.

"I can't be seen with you."

There was a brief silence between them now. Now the woman looked far into the sea and exhaled and brought her eyes back at the man.

"Just so you know, each time you say that, it hurts a teeny bit more," she said to him, demonstrating further by pulling two of her fingers together, leaving only a tiny space between them. There was a kind of slight dullness in her voice now.

"It's nothing…" the man began, almost taking a step closer to her.

"Personal. Yeah, I know. What do you want?" A sharpness lined her words again.

The man heaved a deep breath and sniffed his finger across his nose – the smell of the rotten fish seemed to have finally hit him. He ignored it quickly and said, "If this gets out, I'll be ruined."

The woman cocked a brow quickly. "Wow. Okay. I should've fucking known. How many times must we have this discussion? This is like the umpteenth time, you know," she said, trying and failing to hide the stir of emotions in her voice.

"I don't trust you," came the sharp reply of her companion.

"Calm down. I'm not going to tell the press or anything. No one will know," she told him, shifting her weight to one side.

The man shoved his hand into the pockets of his black linen trouser. He didn't seem to believe that. He shook his head.

"You need money."

And that got the woman flaring.

"Fuck you! Why can't you get it into your dumb fucking head that I want this baby? It's my body. I'm the one that lets you pay to fuck it, remember? You don't have a choice in this," she snapped at him. She had spoken so loud this time that Iman did not have to strain her ears to hear them. It was loud and clear.

"It was an accident," the man retorted, unperturbed by the harshness in her voice. There was pent-up frustration in his voice and if his hands hadn't been in his pockets, Iman would have sworn he was holding them in a fist.

"Accidents happen, sweetie. I hate to be the one to break it to your pampered ass," she all but snarled in his face. After which she reined in her fury.

The man exhaled and took a step closer to her. Perhaps he thought he would be more convincing if she smelt his presence.

"Don't come any closer," she huffed, taking a step backward. She'd somehow let go of her cigarette at one point and now had a palm placed upon her forehead.

"Do you want me to beg, because I will?" The man stopped in his tracks with a pleading expression. His voice had the same plea and he seemed almost ready to fall on his knees right about the second. For whatever reason, he really didn't want the woman keeping the baby.

Iman watched the woman looked up at the sky as another rumble echoed from the depths above. When she looked back at her companion, her gaze was drained of its anger. "It is obvious you do not have anything serious to talk about. I'm leaving. See you around," she said to him before she turned to walk away.

"Don't…" the man spat with a quavering voice.

The woman tilted her head backwards and let out a groan in frustration. Before now, she would have easily stopped to hear what more the man had to say. But she trudged across the sands, oblivious to what was about to hit her.

The man took out a knife from his waistband and clutched it behind him. He wore a pair of black gloves. It was evidently a preplanned murder. But even in the gloves, his hands shook fervidly. Iman saw the knife gleaming behind him in the grey moonlight. Her eyes widened with terror as the man edged closer to the woman. What was about to happen seemed inevitable, and Iman wasn't going to blink so as not to miss anything.

The woman seemed to think otherwise about her leaving. She stopped, but did not look back.

"What else is there to say?" she questioned.

"I have money. You can just take that and leave me

alone," the man said – it sounded more like lamentation.

"I don't want your money."

"Please."

"No!"

She turned around now, but still did not suspect that the hand hidden behind the man had an object that would soon be termed a 'murder weapon'.

"What is wrong with you?" she hissed. "It's not as if I'm going to go declare to the world that it's yours. What exactly is wrong with you?" Instinctively, her hand seemed to move to her belly.

The man did not answer that. He kept mute, but only for a moment. His gaze followed her hand. "Can I at least feel it?" he requested.

"The baby?" The woman looked uncertain and shrugged in her coat. Definitely form the cold this time. Iman herself found herself wrapping her arms close as she remained hidden.

The man took another step closer.

"I told you to stay where you are," she warned.

The man stopped for a moment. He couldn't wait to get closer now and fulfill the one thought in his head right now. It almost looked like an itch he wanted to get over with as soon as possible. She turned, facing the way out of the roofless construction site.

"Please. If there's nothing else I can do, then…"

His voice trailed off to nothing. Silence simmered and strained. The woman's down-turned eyes appeared a bit sloppy now. She was softened. "It's too early. You won't feel anything," she told him. Her hands seemed to struggle to find something to lay upon. A cigarette, maybe. The woman resisted the urge though.

"I know, I just…" he answered quickly.

Now he finally covered the distance between them while. This time, she didn't stop him. In fact, she allowed him place his free hand on her stomach. One of her hands carefully fell on his while he still held her tummy. Iman wondered what she was thinking. Perhaps she thought he was finally coming around and would accept the baby? There was no way she could tell he had a knife behind him, ready to be buried within her. The man shut his eyes and sniffled deeply in readiness for what he was about to do.

"Are you crying?" the woman asked in a soft caring tone.

The man sniffed sharply again. "I'm sorry," he said to her, and it seemed like he meant it. "I can't let you ruin everything."

And with every ounce of courage he could gather, he raised the knife – the woman only saw it gleam in the moonlight in the last second as it made its way towards her stomach. But a burst of reflex wrenched her hands in defense. She grabbed hold of his wrist. Iman felt her heart beat strangely. Her feet refused to move as it all continued to unfold.

A scuffle broke out between them. The man grabbed her by the throat with his other hand, his fingers boring into it, and forced her against the crab boxes, just away from where Iman was. It all crumbled on the ground, making the woman lose her balance and her grip upon his other arm.

"I can't let you do this," he scoffed amidst the heavy breathing and struggling.

One final effort drove the knife right through the woman's belly. She let out a muffled groan, her face twisting to the inevitable. Even so, she tried to fight free. It appeared as though her veins were suddenly pumped with adrenaline. Perhaps she fought so hard to save herself, or for her baby. She stomped on the man's foot with the long, blunt heel of her boots. He growled and released his grip on the knife one time. The knife fell off and landed on the sand, dripping with blood. The man fell on one knee.

Finally getting a chance, the woman hobbled away, pressuring her wound to stop the bleeding. But then, the man, faster than her injured self, dove forward and grabbed her foot. She crashed to the ground, yelping.

"NO!" she yelled.

But the man sensed that someone might come to her rescue if she let out a distress call that was loud enough. He tried to pull her back, but she had her bloody fingers dug into the ground to gain traction.

"HELP! PLEASE! HELP ME!" she let out a call, breathing heavily and fighting even harder.

She quickly made a turn onto her back and shoved her leg in his way, but he dodged it and grabbed the leg. Pinning the other one down on the ground, he pulled up to her height – his whole weight was now on her. And as quickly as he could, he wrapped his hands around her throat to finish her off, dumping any attempt to finish her off with the knife.

She flung her legs in the air and pushed them against the sands as life was being squeezed out of her. Her face had turned reddish purple as she gasped her final breaths. The man gripped the neck even tighter, supporting it with his weight. It was like the more she struggled, the tighter it became, like a noose around a slim neck.

"You made me do this!" he scoffed. His face had gone crimson and the muscles in them was tough and winkled as he squeezed out what was left of her.

While the murder was going on, Iman stole out from behind the crab boxes. Her feet had finally heeded her will. At least, that was what she thought. When she came out, her nose caught the faintest smell of blood and she was once again frozen, unable to move. She was standing some distance away, behind the man. Her eyes and those of the woman met in a faint line. The woman feebly raised her hand for help.

"Help me," she begged – her voice was fading – there was barely a life left in them. Sweat covered her face and tears were formed at the corners of her eyes.

But Iman stood there, watching, not knowing what to do. She was utterly bemused as though she was in some kind of trance.

In one final desperate plea, the woman locked eyes with her killer and said, "Pl--please. St--" The words didn't have the time to come out her mind fully. And one final breath later, the woman stopped moving. Her limbs fell limp and Iman knew… she knew because she'd seen this before. The woman was dead.

The sky rumbled once more, witnessing all that was happening along with Iman. And at the woman's last breath, the sky wept. A drizzle began, too soft to bother anyone, but enough to cause sharp jolts of chilling current run through Iman. But the sky wasn't the only one who wept for the dead woman.

The man slowly withdrew his hands. A cloud of mist gathered over his head, and soon came the tears. It was those of pain and freedom, and perhaps those of remorse. He remained in position for a while, with his knees on the woman's sides quivering – droplets of sweat had formed across the small part of his forehead that was visible.

He then rolled off her to the side and landed in a prone position. He gazed up into the sky. A thousand eyes had been watching his action all the while. It could be out of remorse now that he sobbed bitterly.

Freed from her shock by the rain, Iman quietly backed away and disappeared into the dark. There was a chaos of thoughts in her head now, not making sense. Things were beginning to get blurry to her again, occurring in flashes and bits and with various cuts in time. Iman tried to stop it and that made her let out an involuntary whimper. Wrong decision.

There was suddenly a gust of wind following the sound

she let out, muting the sound a tiny bit. However, the man still felt a presence and then shot up instantly, just in time for Iman to let the darkness of a corner wrap her within its grip. He looked around carefully, and then Iman could have sworn he looked straight at her and saw her standing there in that corner. But his gaze shifted over to another corner at that moment. The only thing was while he hadn't seen her, his shadowed face had been perfectly illuminated by the moon. She saw him.

However, the man surely still suspected he was being watched and that made Iman stay still. Of a sudden, or a miracle, the sky cried harder and the rain suddenly increased in its force. That was what Iman needed to get the hell out of there. The sound of the rain buried every sound that might have given away Iman's location.

And now, Iman sprinted across the beach – arms and legs flailing like windmills, caring not the tiniest bit about the rain that poured from the sky. It had begun to rain even heavier at this time. Flashes of lightening ripped across the clouds and drums of thunder crashed dispassionately. A squalid was rioting far down the beach. But fearlessly, Iman whizzed against the howling wind. The abandoned boat was only a few other boats ahead. She had been drenched already, but the boat was her destination, and she would not stop until she got to it.

Truly, she didn't until she was safe within those walls. That was when Iman herself began to cry.

***

As it rained that night, the rain drenched The Man. He didn't know why he stayed there by the side of the body without moving, almost like a lifeless person himself. Maybe a part of him expected the rain to somehow cleanse him of this great sin he had committed. He couldn't say for sure.

Eventually, The Man left, sparing one final look at the woman he'd killed. She laid there, beautiful even whilst dead and with the rain anointing her body. He almost hated himself for riding the world of suck beauty, but it had been necessary. The rain had surely not washed The Man clean of all sins, but it had done well in taking the smell of blood and sweat off him. Now he needed a place to dry off.

The boat with which he used to arrive was abandoned with the other boats and he walked the rest of the way home. If he was being honest with himself, this was probably his most peaceful of nights. There was no worry about the threat the lady posed to his life. The rain had been quick to subside and he was now simply strolling through the streets of Deira without any care. The city wasn't quite asleep yet. There were still a few people on the streets now which he easily dissolved into. The Man paused in his steps and turned to the right. He was suddenly beginning to crave kebab. With that in mind, The Man made his way into the first shop he saw that sold kebab, smiling broadly.

"Welcome," the bearded, and sleepy, man behind the counter said to him. He leaned backwards as he observed The Man carefully. "You look like you've had quite the eventful night." The other man looked out the window and frowned. "Wasn't it raining? You must be so cold."

The Man smiled, the memory of what had happened tonight almost already forgotten. Almost. "Yes. And for that reason, my friend, you may want to treat me to the very best kebab in all of Deira." The restaurant was pretty much empty save the owner. It was perfect that way.

The other man mirrored his smile though and shrugged. "I wouldn't say it's the best," he said as he proceeded towards the grill. Then he added, "Tell me, how's married life treating you?"

"Just great. I suggest you yourself get a wife, Erol." He sank into the nearest chair and watched the other man do his business while talking about his reason for not having a wife. The Man listened half-heartedly as his mind thought of what the rising of the sun would bring.

Tomorrow, when the city awoke, they would find a beautiful dead woman by the edge of town. And the whole city would be turned upside down in search a killer. They would find one, but it wouldn't be him.

He'd made sure of that already.

CHAPTER SIX

Iman was dreaming again, and the dream was a memory.

She was within the arms of a woman who held a familiar scent; sweets and pastries. Iman sank into the woman's arms as they both remained seated in cushioned seats.

"Why are we going?" muttered Iman, causing the woman to stop humming.

The woman smiled brightly and brought her face to Iman. "A fresh start," she told her. "Away from all the bad things. Sometimes when bad things happen, you just have to stay away from it and find your feet."

Iman looked out the window. They were in a train. That she remembered vividly, and she liked the way the train travelled smoothly, enabling her to observe some parts of her new habitat. The buildings and the people were very different from what she was used to in London. They spoke different to. She didn't know why exactly they were here.

"But why here?" she grumbled to the tired woman beside her.

"You father had some business in Deira before…" She paused and tried on a smile again. "Once we get there, we'll settle."

"In Dira?" said Iman, frowning.

The woman chuckled and corrected her, "Deira." She pulled Iman closer, allowing her sink further into her comforting smell. "If you're bored, you can always watch your cartoons on your iPad. But for now, you should just--"

BOOM!!!

There was a sudden and powerful jolt across the train, followed by screams that seemed to rise from everywhere. Iman's vision spun wildly and she fought to cling on to something while she felt her body being jerked out of the seat. For a moment she felt a hand. A sharp grazing of skin against hers. Then a force yanked her away and her body was bursting through the window she'd been staring at before.

When Iman opened her eyes, she was laying on the floor. Her body was soaking wet and sharp grains of sand dug to her exposed skin. When she tried to get up, she felt sharp pain through her body. Her senses seemed to register the beanie upon her head and the bag slung across her body. She groaned from the pain and attempted to stand up again.

This time, when her body hit the ground from the pain, she realized she was no longer on the ground. Another woman took her place. She had warm toned skin and wide brown eyes that stared back at Iman who was not standing beside her.

The woman was bleeding, her eyes were empty and her lips were chapped.

Slowly, those heavy lips parted and tears glistened around the woman's face as she said, *"Help me."*

Iman felt her limbs frozen in place at the sight of the woman. Her mind screamed for her to help but she was unable to even until the woman choked on her words finally. And in that instant, the woman wasn't the one laying on the ground anymore either. There laid a man with dark eyes.

"I see you," his cool voice said.

***

It was a calm and humid weather this morning, a huge contrast to how Iman felt when he awoke. The sky was clear as if it hadn't almost emptied its reservoir last night. The sun was already out in the horizon. It was starting to thaw.

It had been a raging storm last night, however short it lasted. The result could be seen this morning everywhere; fishing baskets and trampolines were displaced from their original positions – pieces of dead fishes were littered here and there (a little to the glee of those who were packing them into baskets already) – boxes and pieces of papers were thrown across every path. The shore was wet and several parts of the harbor, including the boats were still dripping with water. Some of them were water-logged, especially the areas the fishermen built their tents. The fishing space generally looked more like a public disposal site. But as the fishermen began to tidy their surroundings, there were now some pleasant places to set one's eyes on.

Iman followed the usual exit and squeezed herself out of the abandoned boat. She was no longer bothered that people might see her and ask her to leave the boat. It was her home for now, and she would defend it. *But who would ask her to park out of an abandoned boat anyway?* She thought. The boat itself had had parts of it crashed by the raging storm from last night, especially the windows. As if Iman didn't have enough to be worried about in the first place. But no matter how it looked like, it still provided shelter for Iman – it was still her home. Here in Deira.

Her eyes were heavy, suggesting that she might not have had a good sleep the previous night. Considering the nightmare that hadn't fully eased out of her body, one couldn't quite blame her. Iman still felt a bit of dread and its paralyzing venom. The last words in her nightmare still haunted her, and as she eased herself away from the boat, a part of her kept thinking the man would come after her and silence her.

Iman did her best to control her thoughts despite all that. Still, she found her feet leading her towards a rather specific place.

She squinted and hooded her eyes with her hand as the sun's rays dazzled them. The events of last night were still fresh in her head and the path that led to the warehouse that was being constructed wasn't very hard to follow. She had a feeling that the woman's corpse would still be lying at the scene, and for whatever reason, she was drawn towards it.

A voice caught her attention. She looked around the shore and harbor – the fishermen were fast at work already, speaking loudly to each other in their native tongue. With her hair tucked into her green beanie, she moved, her steps suspicious and her eyes dark. She meandered through the paths, past some of the fishermen and their fishing tools.

She was awfully aware of their gazes following her and she half-expected one to stop her.

They didn't.

Now she was at the crab box storage area. From a distance, she sighted the body of the woman. Truly, she was still lying on the ground, definitely dead. Contrary to Iman's hope that last night would have been nothing but the nightmare it was. But seeing her here in that position and knowing she had not moved, she couldn't keep that hope. Iman, not minding if anyone was looking at her this time padded closer.

The corpse had gone pale and the rigor process appeared to have been completed. She was still pretty even with her facial muscles looking rigid. She had been thoroughly washed by the rain and that made her skin even paler. The blood on the spot she was stabbed had curdled. Beside her was the object that had taken her life. It still had the evidence of blood on it, despite the rain.

Iman crouched beside the corpse to behold that face again. She was amazed at how much she seemed to have changed in just a few hours. *How thin is the line between life and death?* She questioned.

Swallowing, Iman reached forward to touch the woman's face. She had been meaning to do it all along. It felt as though touching it was what would prove to her that this was, or wasn't, the woman she'd come to DEira in search of. Reaching out slowly made the distance between her and the woman's face seem too long. But then someone halted the movement...

"Oi!"

Iman turned around sharply to see a heavily-bearded fisherman. He had a shawl around his neck and looking just like the man she had seen two nights ago. The pair of wellington boots he wore dug into the ground he stood. He did not say another word after he called out to her, but the look in his eyes was as cold as the stiff expression on the face of the dead beside her. It held a dangerous warning.

A bone-chilling sensation coursed through Iman's spine. She quickly surmised that if she remained here, something terrible might happen to her. It was time to get away. It was to run.

She got to her feet. The fisherman kept his eyes on her as she backed away from the corpse. He knew what she had been planning to do to the body, and so he began to walk in her direction. But Iman turned and streaked off in the opposite direction. The man gave his movement some speed as he drew forward. A part of Iman was sure he was coming straight towards her to grab hold of her and blame her for the death of the woman. People were quick to blame people like her for a lot of things, just like the woman at the clothing store had done the other night. She wasn't going to let that happen.

A quick look behind her proved she'd been wrong though. The man had approached the body instead. The man lifted his gaze in her direction and seemed to say something.

But that was not for Iman to hear. She was far gone – sprinting through the maze of crab boxes, ropes, nets and fishing tackle. She looked over her shoulder again – no sign of the fisherman coming after her. Still, she didn't stop in her fleeing. She breezed ahead, panting.

However, she had obviously not been paying attention to the way she'd been going, her gaze still looking behind her just to be sure the man truly hadn't been chasing after her. That was exactly why she saw the stack of crab boxes before her too late. She tried to avoid her impact with it shifted her weight to the left. It hadn't been enough she she'd really only succeeded in tripping. Her feet were dislodged and she crashed pitifully on the ground.

The darkness welcomed her instantly.

CHAPTER SEVEN

If Annie Fakir had known this was how her day was going to go, she would have had breakfast. Instead, she was currently going on with only coffee in her stomach. A quick glance at the time proved that it was 10:34am. A little too early to be dealing with the most massive thing she'd seen though all her time with the Dubai Police Force.

The crime scene was teeming with police officers, clad in their olive green drabs. It had been barricaded with the conventional 'CRIME SCENE. KEEP OFF' yellow tape. Some of the crab boxes were within the barricade, and that meant the owners had lost the right over them for now, not to mention the owner of the construction site where the murder had taken place. Behind the barricade were cars parked here and there. The fishermen and women from the fish market were standing around, drawn by this untypical attention to their settlement, and watching as the policemen observed every part of the scene. The woman's body had been bagged and carried into the ambulance already. The weapon of murder had also been bagged.

Now the siren blared, and the ambulance drove off, leaving the police to do the rest. The coroner would handle things at his side. Here, however, there was still so much to be done. Forensic scientists were taking photos and the detectives were investigating the whole place.

Hanging around the crime scene were members of the press from several media houses – one of which was Light House Media. A camera had been staged and a lady reporter was giving details as much as she had gathered. Annie Fakir couldn't help but listen.

"Hello, world, I am Cindy Williams reporting live from Dubai Creek," the lady began. She was a beautiful dark-skinned woman who was well past her forties and was dressed rather smartly. The smile she wore was a small and practiced thing which Annie found unfitting for the current mood. "Early this morning, the body of an unidentified woman was discovered at the beach. As you can see behind me," she continued, pointing, "the police are here at the scene searching for any clues as to what may have transpired here, although there have already been reports that that the victim was stabbed and strangled to death.

"About an hour ago, Detective Annie Fakir gave an unprecedented press conference in front of a large audience in a town that has never before seen such a brutal crime. We hope that before the end of today, the police will come up with some information as to what led to the death of the unidentified woman or the person that may have committed this dastardly act. Until then, stay tuned as we continue to bring you live updates from the scene. I am Cindy Williams – Light House Media news." The moment she was done broadcasting, her smile got snuffed off her face and Annie shifted her focus. She had enough problem that concerned her at the moment.

Standing beside one of the boats with a police officer and a fisherman. There were onlookers standing by, perhaps waiting to be interviewed too. Annie didn't think that would be necessary.

"Did you notice any uncanny movements here last night?" she asked the older man who stood meekly beside her. He was one of the few people here who spoke English.

"No, I didn't. It rained almost the whole night, and so we were all in our tents. There was no scream or yelling," the man answered curtly.

Annie nodded. That was what she thought. The rain had been the perfect cover for the murder to carry out his plan. "And before this incident took place, have you noticed any strange person or behavior around here? Was there a fight amongst you maybe?" she asked, hoping there would be something that could give her a bearing and direction on this case.

"Not at all! We live in peace here. We cast our nets and set our hooks in harmony. We all have our spaces and we respect each other here. We even help each other. I have been fishing here for a very long time, and not for once have I seen the men here fight over anything. And I don't even think I have seen the women at the market fight. We are all traders and are here for business. It is our only means of survival, so why should we kill each other?" the man explained, a bit confused by whatever Annie implied with her question.

The man sounded so assured that the crime was not from within that Detective Fakir almost believed him. However, in this case, everyone was a suspect, even this kind man.

"Thank you," she said to the man eventually before sending him off.

Reports continued to pour in as the police investigated the scene. Detective Fakir had left the scene. The murder weapon had been sent to the lab for fingerprints matching.

"You know what I think?" said the officer beside Annie with a mouthful. He was a middle-aged man with a rather huge bod, clad in the regular drab. He was also helping himself to a plate of barbecued fish which he carried around as Annie began to move towards her car. Annie knew she wouldn't be able to stop the man from airing his views regardless so she said nothing. "I think it was her husband."

Annie shrugged. "We don't even know if she's married, Hussain," she said flatly, not stopping in her movement through the sand.

"Pretty thing like that? I think she is. She isn't form around here though and she doesn't wear a scarf either. No wonder he killed her," he explained further as he munched on, even spewing bits of fish away.

"You know what, you're probably right, Hussain," Annie said to him once she reached the car. Hussain offered a toothy smile and wore a proud look on his face. Anything to get him off her back. "I'll keep that in mind while I continue with the case. Right now, I need to get to the station."

With that, she opened the door of her car and slid inside it. She didn't hesitate to get the car started and leave the entire place. Soon afterwards, Detective Fakir was back at the station. It was chaos over here. The kind she'd never seen before. There was a mass of press over there, shooting numerous questions her way. Annie stood tall at the entrance of the station, dressed in a white shirt that was open at the collar. It was tucked into her black trouser, making her look more like a banker than a detective. Her raven black hair was tied in a ponytail, exposing prominent cheek bones. There was a look in her face – one that had seen too much in the world of crime and violence.

She was surrounded by the press holding up their microphones and other recording devices as she gave them a briefing on the case. Camera lights flashed from every side. She would probably need to put on her glasses if this interview had taken place in the dark – perhaps, at night. Every reporter would do anything they could to cover the story as this was a crime that had never been seen in this part of Dubai.

"The peace and harmony of our tranquil Creek has been disturbed today," Annie announced, silencing all of them.

There was elegance in her voice. Authority preceded her words – authority to reprimand the offenders of the law in the most brutal way. And it didn't seem like the man, or woman, that had committed the crime had a chance.

"But make no mistake, we will find out who committed this heinous crime. We'd like to start by urging anyone who may have seen or heard anything untoward in the past few days to come forward, please. That is all I have to say for now. Thank you."

Detective Fakir turned away, igniting a flurry of questions from the local journalists. Some of them struggled to reach her, but the other officers standing by held them back.

The questions were thrown at here from the chaos of people who gathered there. These questions and more were asked, but at this time, the detective had no answer for them. And so she walked into the station, escaping the never-ending questions of the press.

***

The case was treated with maximum attention. Detective Fakir had called the lab to know if there had been a fingerprint match, but scientists were yet to come up with something. At this point Detective Fakir had not gotten a lead, and she knew the city was expecting information soon about the killer. That, she thought, would probably reassure their safety. And it would put her mind at some kind of rest. Her mind kept shifting over to the sight of the dead girl she'd seen and Annie felt a wave of nausea. No one deserved that kind of fate; dead in a lonely corner of a town.

Annie was just beginning to get cranky form the frustration of having no leads when Hussain came to her and informed her someone had stepped forward. Annie was up on her feet almost immediately.

"Where is he?" she all but demanded from the older man.

Soon, Annie was striding through a hallway and on her way to the interrogation room. Already, she could see as he sat comfortably in the interrogation room, waiting for the person he had demanded to see. He looked enthusiastic about it, tapping his fingers tentatively on the long silver top table before him. He'd better have good information to offer to Annie.

The door swung open and Detective Fakir walked in. She was followed closely behind by Hussain who allowed his feet drag against the ground as they got in.

"Good day, sir," greeted Annie, walking to the steel chair at the other end of the table. She wiped sweat off her forehead and looked the other man squarely in the face.

Hussain on the other hand stood behind the fisherman lazily. If he was given the chance, Annie was sure he would go find something to eat and abandon her here. However, he was quite needed. If the fisherman that had come forward was at all worried by the presence behind him, he did not show it. He only looked over his shoulder and then back at the detective, also carefully ignoring Annie's earlier greeting.

Detective Fakir did not mind that he did not respond to her greeting, nonetheless. She was more concerned with the information she hoped he had come to give.

After she had kept the recorder she had come with on the table, she looked up at him. He was typically a weather-beaten man. He had chapped lips and deep-set eyes. He was not wearing a shawl at this time. That exposed his scraggly grey beard.

"So, thank you very much, sir, for coming forward to tell us what you know about the murder," Detective Fakir began, straightening and trying on an inviting expression on her face. "Trust me the information you give us now will go a long way towards arresting the suspect."

The man had kept his silence all the while with a tight look up his face. He seemed to have suddenly lost his freedom, but at the same time, willing to tell his story.

"Can you tell me your name, please?" Detective Fakir questioned, trying to ease him into the situation he was currently in.

"My name is Adam Salah," he answered almost immediately – his voice quavered lightly and his gaze unfocused. He cleared his throat then.

But perhaps it was to settle his mind that he proceeded to rest his forearms on the silver table, looking at Detective Fakir as if saying, *"Bring on the questions".*

"Okay, Adam. Please tell me what you about the murder?"

He took a breath and sat and pushed himself forward in the chair.

"I was up at the crack of dawn, as always. I'm a fisherman, of course, and we like to start early. I dressed up in my tent, being careful not to wake up the neighbors – and then I headed down to the shore to pick up some gear. That was when I saw the body... and the girl, I guess."

Detective Fakir frowned a bit. "The girl? What girl?" she asked quickly.

"There was a little girl kneeling beside the body," Adam answered. His face held a gentle frown as though he were remembering something.

"Like how old do you think she would be?" asked Annie. The gears in her mind began to think up ways that information fit. Was it a daughter or something? The woman hadn't particularly looked like a mother but Annie couldn't assume anything.

Adam reclined on the chai, still frowning. He didn't look too keen to provide an answer to Annie's question. But after a moment he proceeded to answer anyway. "I don't know, maybe eleven, maybe twelve. I'll be damned if I knew what she was doing down there. Like honestly, I can't say. Looking at the poor dead body, I reckon. She stretched forward to touch the dead body and then I hollered at her. I was walking closer to the scene when she stood up and ran," he explained further to Annie who nodded. She looked up at Hussain but it didn't seem like he was concentrating.

"And do you think you'd be able to give us a solid description of this girl. It would help us identify her easily," said Annie.

"Oh, I'm not so sure about that, Detective. Like I said, she ran off immediately she saw me coming. I can't say I got a good look at her face." He squinted his eyes and moved his hand to his bearded chin.

"Nothing at all? Not even the clothes she was wearing?" Detective Fakir asked. She leaned forward hopefully.

Adam glanced at the roof and scratched his beard. His face wore a light frown as he tried to remember what that strange girl had looked like.

"Well, I think I saw her in a big, baggy coat and a beanie. One of those knitted ones. Green, I think it was. That's about all I can I remember. That's not exactly our sense of dressing, so I am thinking she isn't really from here," the man offered after moments of thoughts.

There was silence in the room – but it was for a moment. Adam remained reclined on the chair, looking absently at the table.

"I want to know, Adam, said Annie. He looked up at the detective. "Have you seen this girl before around the beach? I mean, does she live in one of the tents or maybe she is the daughter of one of the worker…" Her voice trailed on as she searched within Adan's dark eyes, hoping they'd lighten in a peculiar realization.

"No. She's no one's daughter," he answered firmly just like the other fisherman has spoken to Annie the other time. "And I have not seen her anywhere around the beach before. It was my first time seeing such a strangely-dressed girl at the beach."

Now Detective Fakir leaned forward and hunched her shoulders a bit, pondering over the worlds.

"All right, sir. Like I said, this information will go a long way towards arresting the suspect. The girl in question might not be the real killer, but she might give us some information that might lead us to the suspect. Nevertheless, I'll be in touch if there's anything else. Thank you," she said to him finally.

The detective got up on her feet. She took her phone and walked across the table to the where Adam was. He too was standing now, ready to leave. They both shook hands.

"I'm sorry I couldn't be of more use to you," Adam said.

He sounded sorry indeed, but Detective Fakir was not one to ignore the message when someone was trying to be modest. A light frown twisted her face in.

"Oh… not at all… in fact you have been screamingly helpful. Your information just gave us a head start in this case. I tell you, you're of more use to us than you know. Coming here to tell us what you know about the murder is an act of patriotism. So thank you once again for that," she assured him.

Annie's mouth creased into what looked like a half-hearted smile. But Adam would not understand how much his information meant to her. Hitherto, they were lost over which way to go. Their only means of direction was the murder weapon. They hoped that the murder would have been foolish enough to hold it the knife with their bare hands and not wear a glove. But Detective Fakir couldn't say she had been surprised when she received a message that there were no fingerprints found on it. It told her the killer had planned the murder, and must have also actively tried to cover it up. Though he not getting rid of the body had been a bit strange. Most people would have probably tried to push the dead woman into the water. This one hadn't made any such attempt. The case itself was confusing. It was almost like they had reached the *nadir* of their mission, until Adam showed up.

"Hussain will escort you out of the station," Annie told

him curtly before stepping out of the interrogation room. Hussain grumbled something behind her as he helped Adam out the police station. Detective Fakir was in a whirlwind of thoughts as she made her way towards the office.

Momentarily, she caught a scene in one of her colleague's office. There was a woman sitting across his table who had a notably big nose. She had a very accusing look on her face as she said, "--eve me! She stole from me. I have the CCTV footage to prove it."

"But what exactly was stolen from your shop?" the officer sitting across from her – Annie wasn't sure if his name was Akim or Kazeem – asked with a frustrated groan. He had clearly tried and failed to bore that question into the impatient woman's head.

"It's a very big shop. How am I supposed to know?" snarled the woman.

Annie left while the officer said, "I'll have to see that footage of yours."

After a few steps, Annie was back in her office. She was soon propped up on her elbow on the table, with her hand across her upper jaw.

She only took that position for a while before she stood up and went and stood by the window. She pulled down on a blind to get a look outside. All she saw were people going about their daily lives. She thought that the killer would be among these people. But how would she find her? Which direction would lead her to the whereabouts of this little girl? And what if she was the one that killed the woman? Was that even possible? It was near impossible that an 11-

year old could stab a grown woman – not even at her back, but on her belly – that meant the woman saw it coming. She didn't think this little girl was the killer. But she needed to find her, for she held the key towards catching the suspect. She needed a wash off, maybe that would ease her mind and prepare it towards a dogmatic resolution.

She went to the restroom which was fairly adjoined to a part of her office. It was a bare restroom with faint light, lacking in proportions. But it had all the necessary facilities.

Detective Fakir stood in front of the mirror on the wall over the faucet. She looked at herself for a few seconds and was reminded why she was there. She turned on the tap and cupped her hands in the water. She took a deep breath when she poured the water collected on her face. It was just at the right temperature her body needed to cool down.

She did it again and again, as if hoping it would mystically reveal all she needed to know, and then rested her hands on the faucet while looking at herself in the mirror. She closed her eyes and took a deep, anxious breath. And then she exhaled slowly. It was all to build momentum for the task ahead.

When she opened her eyes, the face she saw in the mirror was hers but looking more resolute this time. It was like she finally found her bearing – like she finally found a way.

Suddenly, the door of the restroom came open and there stood the tall form of the Officer Kazeem… Akim? Annie shook off her uncertainty and looked at him with a frown. "Is there a problem?" she asked.

The officer didn't seem to care about the fact that he'd

walked in on her in the restroom. He held a tablet firmly and marched forward. "A woman who was lodging a complain to me showed me the footage of her store from last night," he explained. Annie folded her arms and shifted her weight to see what the officer was now holding up to her face. "I was looking for something else but guess what I found…"

Right there upon the screen of the tablet was an image of the woman who Annie had seen in a body bag hours ago. Her heart skipped a beat, not simply because of the dead woman who was alive in the image but because of a green beanie that stood out in the same scene.

CHAPTER EIGHT

Iman rolled about on the ground. It was with a lot of effort that she brought herself up to a sitting position. She placed her hand on her head with a deep wince. Her mind was starting to get plagued with pangs of headache, causing her to groan further. Soon, her vision adjust and she took in her surroundings. With the crab boxes stacked high at different locations, it was not difficult to tell that she was in crab box storage area. In fact, a seagull was picking on some crumbs of fish on the ground beside her. She wondered what happened and who had helped her into this place after her graceless tripping earlier. She had actually expected to wake up at the police station. But here she was, confused by whatever stranger might have pieced her up from the beach and place her here.

Slowly, she examined her body. Judging by the dried mud on her body and her clothes, it was safe to conclude she had been lying in the muddy ground for a while now. How strange that no one made any effort to wake her up – maybe no one even came this way. She was simply a thing to be forgotten.

Iman heaved a breath and got to her feet – the headache was pounding hard – it was as if there was a drum party going on in there. A little shaky, she stumbled away. Where she was going at this time, she had no idea. Thankfully, no one had stopped her.

As usual, Iman walked along the streets itinerantly. She looked dirty and unkempt and that drew lots of attention to her. Perhaps not the kind of attention she wanted right now. She noticed people casting mortifying looks at her. She suddenly grew comfortable with that. She wanted to have a look and see what exactly it was they saw.

There was a car by the walkway. She went to see herself in the window. Her reflection did not look good at all, she could tell. She lifted up the part of her beanie across her forehead, revealing a bruise. Little wonder the pounding headache or the biting sensation she had been feeling there all this while. She touched the bruise lightly and winced in pain. She must have hit her head on a rock or something when she tripped earlier. Then, a thought just came into her mind – a destination rather – the only place she felt very comfortable in.

She carefully covered the bruise with the beanie. And one final look in the mirror, she left to where her mind had just produced.

***

Erol was standing behind the counter, watching the TV as usual and chewing a bubble gum. A report was being delivered and he was so engrossed that he didn't want to miss anything.

Shown on the TV was a blurry CCTV still photo of the victim who had apparently been murdered last night. It had been taken while she was in a department store earlier that day, the newscaster had explained. The voice of the reporter could be heard at the background of the photo as she revealed all the other details from the case. Those that were made public, of course.

"...police released this image of the victim which continued to..." her voiced seemed to fade into nothingness in Erol's mind. His chewing had also come to a grinding halt.

Erol gazed fixedly at this face on the screen. Although the image was blurry, the beauty of the woman could still be noticed. A blend of emotions fermented in his mind – that of pity, sorrow and a vial of guilt. There was a certain unsettling look in his eyes which he hoped no one else had noticed. They didn't need to know what he had done.

But it wasn't like there were really a lot of people to see him. And the only one in the restaurant was watching the news report with him. The customer who was watching from across one of the tables, tucking in a kebab was the one whose arrival in Dubai had been mentioned by Fatima days ago. Zeenat's daughter; Janet. She was a chubby young lady, who had just finished her masters in a course Erol had already forgotten abroad, with small beady eyes. She seemed to be a decade or less younger than Erol but since the past few days they'd made acquaintances, they'd found they had quite a lot in common. And she *loved* his kebab so much, much to Fatima's disgust.

"This is awful… and scary too," she commented while chewing slowly. "You know, I came back and this happened. Not the Deira I remember."

"It doesn't seem real to me either," Erol replied, bringing his expression to a controlled one. His hand fiddled with the remote. He couldn't keep looking at that lady's face. It made him feel like all his secrets were laid bare.

"Well, it doesn't matter whether it was real or not. One thing is for sure; no one cares about that hotel anymore," she huffed, smiling curtly. "My mother wouldn't stop complaining about how the hotel is being built with blood money and is a sin."

Erol looked at Janet, redolent of what she had just said. But just at that time, the door jingled and in came Iman. Erol quickly made his decision with the remote and turned off the TV.

"Hey, why did you have to do that?" the woman protested, frowning just a little.

It was like they had been watching something profane – something not appropriate for a little girl like Iman. Or maybe a bounty had been placed on Iman's head or something and he didn't want her to know about it. Erol realized the bad timing of his decision then but shrugged it off. He didn't care. Anything to get that image out of his head.

He was however glad that Iman did not seem to catch him doing that. She was quite skittish already and she would have probably turned back and never returned to the shop. Regardless, he didn't fail to note her eyes had quickly moved towards the TV when she was fully in it. It had always been on anytime she visited, and Erol would be watching as though the government had promised some grant for shop owners who watched reports more often. It made sense for her to find it odd.

"Hello again," he greeted, his face crinkling with a smile and hoping to distract her from that. But then he noticed how shabby she looked. "Goodness me! What happened to you, my friend?" he drawled and walked out of the counter towards Iman.

But she took a step backward. Erol halted. She did not answer the question either but looked as if she never wanted to be there in the first place.

"I think she may have slipped and fell in the sand" the woman observed. She leaned backwards in her chair and continued chewing on her meat slowly.

Erol took his gaze back to Iman and tilted his head to one side. "Is that true?" he asked, his voice had assumed that of a father's. Maybe that was what made Iman give a response finally.

She nodded.

"Oh… so sorry, friend. Would you like to wash clean in my bathroom?" he offered, leering towards the door that led to his conjoined apartment.

Iman hesitated for a while before shaking her head.

Erol breathed down and his shoulders dropped. Janet kept her gaze at Iman. The kind of gaze that made one thing they had done something wrong. Erol almost called out to the lady to wipe it off her face. He didn't break his focus on Iman, who kept her face halfway down and only stole glances at Erol at intervals, though.

"It's all right. I'm sure you can sort that out yourself,"

Erol said finally, trying on his smile once more. "You didn't come over yesterday morning though. Did you find the person you've been looking for?" That part about Iman had not been hard to piece together. She was searching for someone, probably a parent. Or it could have been a cat, who knew?

Iman shook her head.

"Oh. Okay. I'm sorry about that. Do not worry, okay? I believe you will find them soon enough." He winked at her.

He turned to where Janet was still sitting and looking at Iman with the same accusing look in those beady eyes of hers. Was he going to make an introduction as he could see the questions written on the woman's face? Well, it didn't seem like it because he turned and faced Iman.

"Have you come to make an order?" he questioned.

Iman nodded.

"The same as the last time?"

Iman nodded again.

"Okay. Coming right up." Then he strode back to his position behind the counter.

Erol began to plate up a kebab. Iman stood patiently, salivating as the smell of the meat wafted through her nostrils. The woman had stopped looking at her intently at this time, probably more concerned by something on her phone.

"I told you I was the best in town, Janet," Erol gloated, his hands busy. "People come searching from far and near for me. Even Superman isn't as good as I am."

Janet chuckled and ended it with a snort. "Superman doesn't sell kebab, Erol." She turned over to Iman and said, "Don't get used to this junk. It's no good for you." She sounded just like Fatima now.

"Leave her be," Erol snapped.

Whatever piece of advice she was giving apparently made no sense to Iman who simply blinked once and turned back to Erol. All she probably wanted right now was food and upon it were all her senses – this woman's opinion didn't matter at all at this point. Perhaps if she had an alternative she wouldn't be here. Erol didn't think she had an alternative. And she was definitely smart enough to see how completely overrated the fish here was.

"I'm just sayin' she needs to look after herself. Look how beautiful she is, yet unkempt," Janet maintained. She turned to Iman again, drawing her gaze off the phone. "Where are you from, my dear? I don't think I've seen you before. I know I was away for a few years but I should know you."

Iman appeared reluctant, but only for a second. Erol considered stepping in to stop Janet from pressuring the poor girl. However, to his surprise, she spoke.

"Iran," she answered.

Janet's face found a new expression which she shared with Erol. "Iran? Huh. We don't get many of those around here. Do we, Erol?" she intoned.

"Nope," Erol replied with a slightly elevated breathing.

"I moved here with my mum," Iman explained. Erol perked his ears. Her mother. Now, the pieces clicked in his head. He now knew who the girl had been searching for. He was a bit hurt Iman was opening up to Janet so easily unlike with him.

Janet recoiled. She looked up at Erol who still trying to get the Kebab ready. "The only Iranian I knew was that foreign man that lived up near the fire station," she said, squinting in an attempt to jog up her memory. "It was before I felt for the USA." She groaned. "What was his name again?"

"Farid," said Erol flatly.

"Who?" Janet questioned.

"Farid. The businessman. Funny accent. I remember Fatima complained about how he didn't have a wife," he continued. "He was the one who ki--" Erol paused and straightened, looking at Iman. Then he tried again, "He was the one who died four years ago or something."

"Yeah, that's right. Farid. I remember now." Janet nodded carefully, her eyes a bit dull now. "So much really changed since I left."

It for once looked like all the reports Erol had been watching finally paid off. He was on top of the news now and Janet was first in line to disseminate. It made him smile a little.

"Yeah. You know even Ahmed recently got married," Erol told her.

Janet gasped. "No way. The one who sells meat? Fascinating. My mother won't even let me breathe over this marriage thing," she said, laughing softly at her own joke. She turned to Iman. "Welcome to Dubai, sweetheart. I understand that you are looking for your mother. Trust me you will find her soon enough, just like Erol had just said."

Iman did not reply to that. She was waiting for her prize. Janet got back to her kebab.

And after what seemed like forever, Erol handed Iman her kebab.

"Here you are."

Iman held the kebab in her hand and gazed at Erol. Iman realized then that Janet was eating and she was not the first customer of the day unlike in their agreement. Erol found it easy to read her tiny reactions sometimes, just like now. He reckoned she thought the agreement they had about him giving her free food had expired. She probably thought he would demand for payment. Erol grinned further, something he'd been doing quite a lot for the past few days. He made the sibilant sign of whispering.

"Our little secret," he whispered.

And for the first time, Iman grinned at him. Erol thought it was beautiful to see her like that. It was the best expression her face had ever produced since he met her. She had a perfect set of white teeth. The smile was rightly made for her face.

"Thank you," Iman appreciated.

They exchanged goodbyes and she left. He knew Iman probably thought highly of him, many people did. His eyes moved back to the TV and he wondered what they would think when they knew what he'd done.

CHAPTER NINE

A thousand eyes twinkled in the night sky over the Canal. Detective Annie Fakir had just arrived at a small, *bistro-esque* restaurant. She wore a livid combat and a black Denim jacket – behind the jacket was a black shirt. On her head was a baseball cap – all giving her that bad girl feeling.

The door slid open as she walked in. The restaurant was buzzing with life. Some of the tables were taken by classy people who were sipping on some wine, eating and conversing – all in the mirth of a cheerful night. There was soul music playing in the background, and those who weren't talking had something to bob their heads and slap their feet on the ground to.

Annie scanned the room. Her presence by the door caught some attention – but she was seeking that. And just right across the left side of the room was the lady she was looking for. She was sitting alone at the table.

Now she walked towards the table. She'd noticed some of the men had stopped to admire her shapely figure and the pride with which she carried herself. Some of them may have recognized her as the lady keen on protecting the image of their neighborhood. That was if they looked past her ass. Annie shuddered. As much as she hated those gazes, she was quite used to it and found them easy to ignore.

At the table was a lady just as attractive as she was, albeit clearly not a native of this land. She had blonde hair, and bright blue eyes that declared her British ancestry. Her skin gleamed in the strobe lights overhead, and her eyes twinkled as she saw the detective coming her way.

"Wow. Look at you," she crooned like a mother to her little daughter. An easy smile fell in place upon her face.

"Sorry I'm late," Annie apologized, the expression on her face was more inviting than what she was forced to present back at the station. It was her other side that was hardy seen by others. Annie found it fitting. These were two worlds of her life that were very much different in many ways.

A smile warmed up to her face too as she reached the table that'd been reserved for the both of them. The other lady stood up and pulled her into a warm hug. They kissed each other on the cheek. But over the lady's shoulder, the Detective Fakir caught the eyes of one of the people in the restaurant. He was gazing at them. Annie's mind instantly pulled up a box to classify him into as she scrutinized him – fancy hairstyle and a flirtatious look. His shirt was buttoned halfway, exposing his hairy chest for whoever cared to look. Their eyes immediately met, the man looked away. Detective Fakir did not react to that. However, the look on her face was a message direct and deep enough for him to understand.

Back off.

Once they broke the hug, she pulled back the chair and sat down. The other lady, who hadn't noticed the silent threat Annie gave the man, sat down too. It was like they had come for some peace talk.

"So what's up?" the lady asked while they waited for the order. She effortlessly pulled a wave of her blonde hair behind her and pulled her lips into a seductive smile. Even the way she rearranged her posture in the chair was flirtatious.

"Nothing, really," Annie answered. There was a glass of water on the table and she helped herself to it quickly.

The lady gazed at the detective, her interrogatory eyes boring through her in search of something more meaning than *"Nothing, really"*.

"I would've understood if you wanted to take a rain check," she finally said to Annie, the edges of her lips faltering.

"No, no, Eliza." Annie dropped the glass and shook her head. "I needed to get out," she added with an affirming nod.

Eliza took a sharp breath. She had given up on the questions and soon assumed a more caring disposition. "Dare I ask how your day was?" she said.

A gentle smile escaped Annie's lips. It was probably due. Her day had taken a far more drastic turn than she would have ever dreamed of. She leaned back against the chair as if she had been asked a question too heavy to answer.

"It is unbelievable... horrible, but just... I dunno. The only thing this place has ever had to deal with for the past fifteen years was Chavs setting fire to dustbins and the occasional fight on Friday nights. And now all of a sudden this happens. I mean what the hell! Murder! There's no way I'm ready for this. I'm just not ready," Annie found herself lamenting to the only one who would understand.

Just as she dropped the last word, a waiter came to their table – a young boy most likely in his twenties.

"Good evening, ladies," he greeted.

Eliza turned at him with a tight smile. "Hi," she responded.

But Annie was not out for pleasantries. The look on her face simply told the waiter not to look her way. Her thought had actually left the scene to the more practical aspect of the case already, and she'd quickly built back the walls in her demeanor.

"Can I start you off with a bottle of wine? Still? Sparkling?" the waiter asked. His smile was a charm in the lights. Eliza must have nodded because then he said, "Is there anything else you would like then?"

"I think just the wine list for now," Eliza answered.

"Very well."

The waiter withdrew from the table. Eliza looked at her companion, Annie. She seemed absent minded. Then Eliza stretched forth a hand and too the one Annie left on the table. It was such a simple action others wouldn't notice. That gently contact of skin on skin made an easiness settle within Annie. However, they broke the contact soon enough when someone walked past their table and Eliza straightened.

After a few seconds of silence, Eliza said, "So, um, I don't mean to be out of line but... do you have any idea who she was? I mean the victim." Annie didn't miss the unsteadiness in Eliza's voice as though she was asking something she wasn't supposed to. Then she smiled to ease the other woman.

"She was a sex worker, we think. No ID. No address. Not even a phone. That's about all we've got aside from a weapon at the scene but... no prints," she explained.

"Jeez! Now I understand why you're this frustrated. It's a dead end."

"Not to mention the storm last night. Our only real lead is a footage from a store but an officer is trying to see if we can get more footages from surrounding places that tells us what happened after she left the store," she explained further, gently leaving out the detail of the girl in the green beanie. Annie was hoping it had been a coincidence that the girl had been with the woman at the store and at the beach after the murder. She was having a hard time convincing herself that was the case though. If only she'd find her. Groaning, she dropped her head on the table sheepishly. "What do I do, Eliza?"

Detective Fakir was down in the dumps. Having no lead in a case was quite frustrating. Adam may have been up and patriotic, but there was still more to the case than met the eye, she thought.

Then Eliza reached across the table and gently pulled Annie's left cheek, causing her to smile. Then she slowly nudged her head upwards. "You breathe, you clear your head and you find the monster that did this," she advised.

Detective Fakir eventually caught her breath. The gentle touch from Eliza seemed to work the magic. She swore, she could have sunk into Eliza's touch forever and even proceeded to stretch her hand forward. And just at that time, the waiter showed up again with the wine list. The detective gently withdrew her hand as he passed the list to Eliza.

"Here we are."

"Yeah, thanks," Eliza said.

"I'll be back shortly," he added.

He left again. Eliza glanced down the wine list. It was not clear what her thoughts were. But then suddenly she heard a raucous laughter across the other side of the room. She looked up from the paper. It had come from the table of the rosy-cheeked playboy. She caught him stealing glances at them. She wondered what would have made them laugh like that. Detective Fakir also looked in their direction. Just like Eliza, she also wondered what the laughter was all about. But she didn't allow that get into her head. She had more frustrating thoughts in there already.

"Can we just not talk about it for a while, please? For tonight, at least," she requested.

"I'm sorry. Of course," Eliza replied.

She gazed at the detective for a while and then returned to the wine list. However, she at short intervals, she stole glances at her. She noticed she was sort of fidgety, shuffling in her seat and sighing repeatedly.

***

After their time at the restaurant, Annie and Eliza strolled hand in hand across the street, shooting the breeze. They appeared more like sisters than what they actually were. It was not acceptable in any form in this town. Annie Fakir might be a detective – a dedicated one at that, but it would not be safe if others found out about her relationship with Eliza. It was however, a risk she was willing to take. Eliza too was just as eager.

They were walking past the cinema on the other side of the road. It had been a lonely silence between them for a while. Eliza thought it was time she broke it.

"...you still haven't told them?"

Detective Fakir turned at her. She was surprised that she would even ask such a question.

"Are you serious? You don't know my parents. They would freak. Especially my dad. You know this thing..." she paused for the tiniest moment before continuing, "...what we have isn't acceptable in this part of the world."

Eliza nodded, but Annie saw the dejection in her eyes. "Are you guys close?" she asked.

"Not exactly. We speak. But we clash. A lot. It's a generational thing." Annie shrugged, the very thought of her father causing a stir of annoyance.

"Traditional?"

"That would be an understatement."

"Gotcha!"

They both chuckled. The night sky was a perfect sensation.

But as they walked past the cinema, Detective Fakir suddenly stopped like one that had been struck by a freezing spell. Eliza was shocked to see her like that.

"What is it?" she asked.

Right there, a little distance from where they stood, the detective had just seen the last person she had hoped to see tonight. The girl in the green beanie. She was coming out of the cinema, her green beanie visible in the entrance lights. Annie unlinked hands with Eliza and that detective side of her kicked in at once without much effort. She kept her eyes on the young girl, memorizing every inch of her face, while walking towards her.

"Annie," Eliza called from a few paces behind the detective.

"One second," Detective Fakir answered in a sharp whisper, careful not to draw any attention form the unsuspecting girl.

Annie paid mind to her steps. She wanted to move as unsuspecting as possible so as not to attract the girl's attention. The girl herself traversed along the walkway, oblivious to what was going on.

There was a break in the traffic. Annie hastened her movement a bit across the road to a space in the middle. A few cars whizzed by, and when it was all clear, she realized that the girl had disappeared around the corner as though she were a spirit. Annie wasn't quick to throw out her search. She was certain the girl was still somewhere around – after all, she had not noticed that she was being followed. Detective Fakir crossed the rest of the road and went after her.

She reached the corner she thought she had last seen a trail of a green beanie, but there was no sign of her.

"Where the hell did she go?" she hissed sharply to no one. A cuss followed her words soon afterwards.

Annie looked around again, behind the waste bins and dark enclosures. But she did not find her. She had thought for a moment that her worries were over. That girl would have been the perfect prize this night if she had caught her. But luck was never on Annie's side. A part of her suspected that the little girl may have noticed that she was after her. However, if that was the case, and she tried to escape, then she might actually be the killer she had been looking for, she thought. There was a strong possibility building in her that that girl in the green beanie might have had a hand in the death of the woman. Annie recalled that her movements were too creepy, too swift for a girl of her age. She laid her resolution to the fact that she had to find her.

The little girl was the key to solving the case.

***

Iman's evening had been quite eventful. She'd found a poster of a horror movie that would be shown at the local cinema and had found a way to sneak in and watch. It hadn't been quite scary, as she'd hoped, but the powerful speakers in the dark room had absolutely thrilled her.

That had been a while ago and Iman was still smiling as widely as she had been back then as she went home. Iman had just arrived at the path leading down to the crab box storage area. The streets may have been lighted up, dispelling much of the darkness. But it was thick dark here. The silence that existed was only broken by the buzzing of the crickets and other insects.

However, even in the dark, Iman could make out a policeman in a reflective coat standing guard up ahead. Iman froze at the sight of him. The policeman did not see her. But a lot of thought flickered into her mind regarding what would happen if he did. She hadn't been aware of where she was right until now. The yellow tape caught her attention and then the smell of the rotten fish.

Her mind conjured up sights of a body wearing the face of a beautiful woman. Blood. And the fisherman who had seen her.

That was all the reason she needed for fear to worm into her heart as if being pumped by her veins. They were coming for her, she was sure. She quickly dived for cover behind a fishing shed. But she had pushed herself too frantically that she knocked over a spade leaning against the fishing shed. The spade clanged ceremoniously against the ground – so loud it almost woke up everyone around. And that of course, caught the policeman's attention.

He flashed his torchlight in her direction.

"Who's there?" He had spoken first in Arabic before adding this in uneven English.

But Iman remained silent, her heart pulsated behind her chest like a speaker diaphragm. She was in trouble now. And she heard it – she heard the officer's footsteps crunching against the gravel as he walked on them, his flashlight scanning the area. He was coming her way. If she made the wrong move, he would see her and that would be the end. Her search for her mother would be halted and who knew what fate awaited her at the hands of these people.

"Whoever you are, beware that this is a crime scene. Trespassing is not allowed here. This area is highly out of bound. Your presence here could put you into serious trouble. You might be tagged a suspect," she heard the policeman warn. His torchlight penetrated nearly every direction.

It could have been out of reflex that Iman crept around to the other side of the shed just in time for the policeman to shine his flashlight at the direction she was hiding.

She was scared. She shut her eyes tightly and held her breath. Was he coming? She might probably let out a scream if she felt a touch this moment. Goosebumps were on her skin and her body shivered.

The flashlight swiveled in the opposite direction and

then the footsteps faded away. It was over. He was gone. Regardless, she listened out carefully for traces of a presence or any sort of movement, but the sound had faded. She was all alone.

Iman could have eased herself out then. But the movies she had watched less than half an hour ago reminded her that the silence could be a ploy to lure her out of her lair. And so she remained in position for a while. The silence deepened. There was no sign of the policeman anywhere around. Iman concluded he must have moved to another part of the storage area.

She peeked out her head and looked around. There was a resolution in her mind that it was safe now. What followed was a deep breath of relief.

She stole out of her hiding place and scurried forward while looking out in every direction for the officer. Her boat was only a distance away. She feared the officer might pop out from somewhere and nab her. The breath that had been of relief was now of fear.

But eventually, she made it to the boat. She hopped across the fuselage and up into the cabin. She found her way into the boat, into her 'grand parlor'. She groped about in the dark and then found her usual spot.

She curled up in a ball on the floor, shuffling around to try and get somewhat comfortable. Iman still felt the fear in her veins, even more than what horror movies usually conjured within her. She didn't like the feeling. But wasn't that the reason she always watched the scary movies? They were supposed to scare her. They were to make her scared of men with chainsaws and monsters with rows of sharp teeth. That fear, and those images were the only distraction from the things that really terrified her simple mind.

Her memories.

Safe now, Iman nestled her head in her arm and slowly drifted to sleep, bracing herself for the horrible dreams that would come. The memories.

CHAPTER TEN

Again, Erol was watching the TV. His restaurant was filled with less than ten people this afternoon which was some kind of progress. They'd all been served and were happily eating away while Erol kept his even gaze upon his television set.

"The mystery behind the brutal seaside killing that has brought not just the area of Dubai Creek, but the entire nation, deepened today when an autopsy report revealed that the victim who was a sex worker was pregnant at the time she was murdered," the hijabed woman onscreen narrated. Beside her, the blurry photo of the woman in the department store captured from the CCTV footage was displayed onscreen. "Despite releasing this photo, the Dubai Police Force of Naif Police Station still have no leads as to who she might be, leaving many with a multitude of theories and burning questions. We took to the streets to find out your thoughts on this utterly gripping case."

The video cut to a series of quick-fire interviews with local residents who had been stopped on the streets or malls, a microphone and printout of the CCTV image brandished across their faces.

A woman wearing a *niqab* and who had an unnecessary apron (in Erol's opinion) stood outside her shop, eagerly waiting to be interviewed. Well, her face wasn't revealed to show that eagerness but from the way she stood, Erol could easily make that conclusion.

"What do you think about this case, madam?" the reporter on set, a young man in a shirt and trousers, asked.

"I have lived here all my life. I have never seen her before, probably because she was always working the night shift, if you know what I mean…" Her voice held a judgmental tone. Erol shrugged.

Another interview quickly followed. A bald boy in a tracksuit who stood by his bike with a girl. "Looks like my dad's ex. Total nutcase," he commented, having looked at the image that was brandished before him. He held a look of disgust.

"Really? What do you think happened to her?" the reporter asked.

"I don't know. Last I heard, my father, just got out of jail. I wouldn't be surprised if the baby was his. You should ask him."

In quick succession, the next interview popped up. A brunette, stifling and wiping a tear from her eye as she held the photo in her quivering hand. "Sorry, it just breaks my heart, you know…" She turned quickly away from the camera.

The next interview made Erol's heart skip a beat. A familiar face stared back at him. A dirty, gaunt, man with a stubble across his chin – he wore a trucker cap. The reporter held up the photo in front of him. He leaned closer to get a proper look.

"Nope. No idea," he said sternly, his American accent heavy upon his tongue.

The reporter wasn't satisfied with that as he'd been with the questions of the others he'd interviewed. "Does this in any way affect the construction plans for the new hotel, Mister Bloom?" the reporter questioned.

"I, err… I'm not going to talk about that," the man answered wearing a gently frown. He looked more than ready to get out of that scene.

"But why? Is it not true that your firm has recently been hired in the construction of that hotel?" he pressed on.

Mister Bloom snapped. "A woman was murdered, for Christ's sake and--" His words had been cut off abruptly as the TV suddenly fizzled out.

Only then did Erol break his gaze and let out a breath. He straightened and looked over to the socket the TV had been connected to. The tiniest wave of smoke hissed from the plug. If Erol didn't know better, he would have called it a bad omen. Maybe it was just Fatima's superstitions rubbing off him or it was indeed a sign.

A sign that the unsuspecting people in the neighborhood would soon realize his involvement in this case.

None of the people in the restaurant reacted to the TV getting stopped that suddenly, so Erol decided to simply pull the plug out of its socket and leave it to be fixed later on. He wasn't sure he was interested in watching more of the news anyway. Still, his mind kept conjuring images of that man in his head.

Shrugging all the thoughts out of his system, Erol still feared the neighborhood was no longer safe. His mind now conjured up a new image. A particular young girl with the most daring brown eyes. If he that owned a shop and had a place to lay his head was worried of how unsafe the area was now, then what about Iman who had nowhere but only slept around in the streets? He thought. He feared for her and hoped he would make a proposition next time he saw her.

He would be better if he knew she was safe. But was she safe here with him, especially if light came to his little secret?

***

Another sun had already set and the case was still not solved. This didn't make Annie happy in any way. However, the detective seemed to have gotten something to feed her hunger for a lead in the case. She was in her house, sitting at the large wooden dining table. She wore pyjamas of thin silk. The short and button-up short-sleeved shirt brought the sexiness in her at first glance. Her curves of fine craftsmanship were outlined carefully in the pajamas. Her bottom was carefully accommodated by the chair as though it was made solely for it. Those were far form the last thoughts on her mind now though.

On the table was her laptop. An array of case documents were littered next to it and all around the table. A glass of wine rested on a coaster to her right. She already knew it was going to be a long night.

All her attention was focused on the laptop screen, clicking from one folder to another. Thanks to Officer Kazeem (she'd finally figured out his name) who'd gone around to retrieve CCTV footages from all neighboring buildings, they had some lead. Except Annie now had to go through every one of them to trail the movement of the dead woman. And she had been doing just that for the past hour.

The folder she had just clicked on now brought her to the blurry CCTV footage of the woman. It showed her walking along the streets. This was quite a distance from the clothing store and the footage had been gotten from a paranoid and racist white man who lived there and was in constant fear of getting attacked. It was dark and so she could not make out much of her. The woman's back was facing the camera. But Detective Fakir needed not worry about seeing her face. Of course, she knew it was her.

There were about a dozen folders with footages from this time frame on her system. Most of them hadn't shown the woman except three Annie had extracted. She'd labelled them *Cam 1*, *Cam 2* and *Cam 3* respectively. She was currently going through the second one. And eight minutes into it, she realized it had just shown the woman walking along the streets. After about three minutes after the woman's form became out of sight, Annie saw the girl in the green beanie trailing the same path. It was safe to say the girl had been stalking her just like it had seemed in the first footage of the clothing store. However, the owner of the store seemed convinced the girl had been there to steal.

"What are you up to?" muttered Annie to herself after going through for footage for the fourth time. She eventually cancelled that one and moved to the third file.

This one showed the woman unlocking her front door. Now, they knew where she lived, at least. Another lead. At the corner of the screen, the little girl's green beanie could be seen sticking out from the shadows. Detective Fakir leaned in, adjusting her glasses. She clicked pause and zoomed in. Iman's figure was blurry but visible behind a lamp post.

Annie took a sip of the wine, kept the glass back on the coaster and leaned back in her chair. Her mind fused the blurry face into a clearer one form the mental image she'd captured. It was the same girl Adam talked about – the same girl she saw last night. She clicked her fingers thoughtfully on the laptop, gazing at Iman's blurry photo.

"Who the hell are you?" she questioned, but the photo did not say a word, unsurprisingly.

She continued to tap her fingers on the laptop impatiently. Everything pointed back to this little girl, but it still made no sense. Her mind began to think of the best way to find her. She could not stop wondering what the girl was doing close to the body as Adam had told her. Perhaps the dead woman was her mother, she thought. Perhaps someone had attacked them that night, and maybe her mother sent her to safety and was killed. And then maybe she returned that morning to behold her mother lying dead on the ground. It was only natural that she had tried to touch her.

Although the image she had on her screen gave a different perspective, there was no way she would give in to the thoughts that Iman actually murdered the woman. She no longer judged her size on hearsay. She had seen her physically and there was no way, such a little girl would stab an adult to death and even strangled her.

However, this image in front of her appeared like this strange girl had been spying on the woman. It appeared like she had been keeping tracks of her movements. And maybe she gave the information of the woman's whereabouts to the person that actually committed the murder. If that was the case, then the girl in the green beanie was an accomplice and must be found.

Annie reached for her phone quickly. A few taps later and she soon had someone on the other end. "Hey, Kazeem. Sorry to bother you so late but can you help me find the address of that house?" she said. She nodded to the officer's response and followed it up by saying, "Yes, the one in the footage." A minute later. "Thank you." The phone was dropped carelessly as she kept her eyes glued upon the image before her.

Detective Fakir's hypothesis would cling in her mind throughout the night. But for now, she was thirsty again. She reached for the wine and drank gracefully.

CHAPTER ELEVEN

A Ferris wheel turned. A pirate ship swayed. A rickety old roller coaster chugged along. The fair was empty.

Iman wandered around, eating from the big bag of candy floss she had gotten from Erol. He had asked her how she was coping with the insecurity in the town and if she would like to come and live with him. But she had turned down the offer, much to his disappointment. The abandoned boat may not be so comfortable, but Iman had her peace. She feared a situation that would remind her of what she suffered in the hands of her previous guardian, after the train incident with her mother. Erol may have presented as a nice person, but she would not trade her peace of mind with sentiments.

As she traversed the path, her attention was soon drawn to a young couple. They were standing by a locally-made merry-go-round. They were waving at their daughter each time she passed on one of the unicorns. The little girl's father ran around with her as they laugh and then he feigned running out of breath, falling on his knees and grasping his chest.

When the ride stopped, the man took his daughter in his arms and lifted her off the ride. The mother took the little girl by the hand and they left.

It was a sight to fancy. Iman watched them walk away while she clung on to her bag of candy floss. She wished she was with her parents. She wished she was with her mother. This scene that had just ended before her was a better motivation. It strengthened her to keep looking. It was a sign of hope that she would find her mother someday.

She walked from one end of the fair to another. Now she got to the token kiosk. She met a skinny boy sitting in the token kiosk. He barely looked up when Iman approached.

"Excuse me," she called.

"Uh-huh," the boy responded, still head bent on what he was doing.

"I lost my mum," Iman blurted.

And now, the boy looked up at her. His countenance took a different color – that of curiosity. He rolled his eyes.

"Name?" he inquired.

She was a bit confused which one it was he was asking for; her mother's name or hers? But she thought it could be hers.

"Iman," she answered.

"Iman what?"

"Mehrabi."

"Huh?" His face creased with confusion – he didn't seem to have heard that name before.

"Mehrabi," Iman repeated.

There was a sudden glimmer of hope in her voice. With the fair full of people, she nursed the feeling that her mother would be one of them. She was looking far down the space now.

The carny picked up a microphone and cleared his throat. There were static and screeches. His voice echoed across the fairground. "Can Iman's mother please come to the kiosk? I'm talking about Iman Meh… Meh--" He turned back to Iman, his face twisted into a very confused frown. "What?"

"Meh-ra-bi," Iman replied in careful syllables. She couldn't even be pissed off right now, given how hopeful she was.

"Iman Mehrabi," the boy said then, smiling tightly. "She's right here waiting for you." The carny put down the microphone and sat down lazily. He then found his fingernails worthy of more attention than Iman herself.

Iman turned back to the landscape of the carnival to see if anyone would come forth. How disappointed she felt that no one came forward. But she waited regardless. In fact, she was ready to wait. And maybe pressure the carny to make the announcement even when there would barely be anyone left at the fair.

The fair got a little busier in time – crowds of teenagers and families making the most out of their time in the last days of November. The colorful fairground lights flashed in all directions and cheesy club music played way too loud.

Iman was still standing by the side of the kiosk, her bag of candy floss now empty, yet she held it in her hand. She was still hoping that someone would answer the call. She was still hoping that a woman would run to her and hug her and ask her where she had been all this while and tell her that she had missed her so much. She thought about how she would revel in the smell of the sweets and pastries and forget all about the past year. If only she could just close her eyes and open it back to see it was all over. And her mother would just appear right in front of her. She was getting tired of looking. How come it was that of all the people here, her mother was not among them? Now she had to watch families play together. It was depressing.

Her mother had said they were coming to Deira for her father's business before the train tracks were blown up. It's been a year now and Iman was still waiting for her in Deira. She felt her eyes redden, and sniffed carefully. She wasn't sure how long she could wait. Was there even some-one to wait for? What if Iman had been the only survivor on that train?

The carny drew in his cigarette and puffed a cloud of smoke in the air. Iman didn't mind – she passively took in the smell.

A man walked by at that moment. He was wearing a trucker cap down low and facing the ground as he walked, with his hands in his pockets. As he walked past the kiosk, the carny spat on the ground, barely missing his shoe.

"The hell?" the man cried out.

But the carny made no attempt to apologize. Instead, he gave him a derisive look and returned to his smoking spree. The man wanted to say something as he was now gazing at the carny.

"What?" the carny asked in a threatening tone. It was now the case of an older man being bullied by a younger man. But the man probably saw no sense in the fight and walked away. The carny took the last drag of his cigarette, and threw what was left of it on the ground, stamping it with his feet.

"Fuck!" he exclaimed. He had obviously been waiting for the man to say something so he could pounce on him. He seemed to know him.

Iman had been watching all that was going on. She felt what the carny did was not right. But at the same time, she could not take her eyes away from the man. She watched him disappear into the crowd.

"When you get older, stay away from creeps like him," the carny advised, leaning back against the chair.

Iman in no way responded to that. She still had her eyes amongst the crowd of people.

And then the carny reached into his pocket and took out a few fair tokens. He turned them around in his hand as if reluctant to part with them.

"Here," he said. "Knock yourself out."

Iman turned. She knew what they were for. And perhaps this would lighten her mood. She opened her palm and the carny dropped the tokens on it. After he had done this, he went back into the booth. It was like he had just paid for the time Iman had spent there with him. Or perhaps it was for the inhaling the smoke from the cigarette without complaining.

Iman left the booth to the Ferris wheel. She had secured herself a space with the tokens. Now she sat alone as the wheel rotated. Other kids had gone.

As the wheel ascended, she looked out over the bright lights of the Canal. She looked up to sky – tiny buttons of stars twinkled up there. She tried to fight back the tears that had welled up in her eyes – biting her bottom lip and wiping her eyes. Heavy breathing and gentle sobs followed. Her heart had longed to do this. It had longed to let it all out. A cloud was gathering just above her head and the tears it produced was bitter and heartbreaking.

"I miss you," she whispered.

And after she had said this, it rained on her cheeks – it was torrential. It was uncanny. It was consuming. Her eyes gave off their relieving waters. This would probably give her a new feeling and strengthen her resolve to keep look-ing till she found her mother.

The thoughts in her mind did not weigh down the Ferris wheel. It continued to turn. The lights in the fair adorned the night sky in perfect iridescence. The cheesy club music resounded across every corner. There were faint screams punctuating the music as the roller coaster chugged in the distance. It was a night Iman would likely not forget in a hurry.

Especially since a police man now stood at the bottom of the Ferris wheel in that familiar olive green uniform. Once the ride stopped, he would take Iman away.

CHAPTER TWELVE

If Erol knew the first person he was going to see at his shop today, maybe he wouldn't have opened. It was at dawn. He had just eased himself into the door and was beginning to approach the double wooden doors of the restaurant and he was tidying up the place, grateful no one had arrived to disturb his peace this morning.

Suddenly, a knock came at the window. It was quite loud he jumped up like a startled rabbit. But then he held his breath and said, "Sorry, I don't open until…"

His voice trailed away to nothing when he saw who was at the window. It was Detective Fakir, holding up her badge. Erol easily recognized her from the news. Her face showed no sign of cheerfulness, which could only mean she knew.

"May I come in?" she asked curtly.

"Of--of course," Erol stuttered. He dropped his broom and made his way quickly to the door to open it up for her. He stepped aside to let her through.

The detective walked like she owned the place, looking around the restaurant as if she expected to find something. Her feet led her all the way to the counter while she remained silent, and Erol knew--*he knew!*--she was looking at his set of knives. Seemingly unsatisfied with her search, the detective turned back to face him.

It was only then he called up the courage to ask, "How may I help you?" He tried to keep his voice even. For all he knew, she was here for a different reason. Perhaps she would like some kebab?

"Are you the owner of the house at No. 54 Chapel Park Road?" she inquired, looking at him like she was going to arrest him for breathing.

Erol sighed. Of course she wasn't here for kebab. She was here because she'd figured it out. "Uh-huh. It's one of my projects," he answered as carefully as possible. "I redo houses from time to time and resell them. I have a few around town. I haven't touched Chapel Park in a couple of years now," he added.

"And you were not aware that someone was living there?" Detective Fakir asked, her expression still blank.

"No, I…" He licked his lips as he tried to find words.

The detective didn't give him a chance. She took a step forward. That step had been threatening; a warning for him not to consider telling a lie. "It has come to our attention that the woman that was murdered on Wednesday night was residing in your property, sir. Are you sure you weren't aware of that?" she said.

Erol took a deep breath. It looked like he had been busted. He reached for the door and locked it. "Come on," he gestured Detective Fakir to a table inside the shop.

They both sat down. The detective did not take her eyes away from him.

"I met her maybe a year ago on my way home from work," he narrated. "She was broke, living in the streets. I just wanted to help her…"

"Did you…?" Detective Fakir interrupted. It was like she thought Erol was going to lie.

"No. God, no! I would never," he protested descriptively, straightening too. Erol wasn't as religious as most people, but he still didn't find sense in making use of a sex worker for any reason. His mother would roll in her grave if that happened. "I let her stay at Chapel Park and that was it. The place was a dump, but a roof over her head at least. It was only supposed to be for a couple of weeks until she found her feet or something." Maybe she had bewitched him like Iman had the other day, or maybe Erol just couldn't stand to watch strays on the street.

"But she stayed," said Detective Fakir.

"I had some financial issues and my mother had just died. I turned my focus at keeping the restaurant running, and before I knew it, a year was gone by. There was no point kicking her out," he explained further.

Detective Fakir nodded in understanding.

"I'd seen her sometimes at the shop. She was loud. Obnoxious. Always grateful, though. I liked her a lot," he said as he conjured up memories. He hated to admit he also didn't want people to know he had any relation with her. News spread trickily in these parts.

If only Iman was here, she would have seen this face of Erol that she had not seen before. It looked pleading, innocent. He wanted to tell the story as pitiful as he could so as not to get those pair of steel around his wrists.

"What was her name?" Detective Fakir inquired.

"I only knew her as Crystal," Erol answered.

"Did you know she was pregnant?"

He shook his head and scratched his beard, uncomfortable at the thought and maybe at the question too. How could he have known if she was pregnant or not?

"I don't understand why anyone would do such a thing to her," he said quietly. The images from the TV came to mind and he felt anxiety over him. The reality of her murder terrified him more than he liked, and it especially made him scared for Iman.

Detective Fakir still carried that blank expression. She was not pleased with Erol and she did not hesitate to let him see it on her face.

"You should've come to us sooner, Mister Bilginer," she said firmly.

Erol dropped his head in shame, tapping his finger quietly on the table. "It took a while for me to process the whole thing," he said. It was enough that he didn't get enough customers. If people knew his relations to a sex worker – no, a murdered sex worker, they would avoid him like the plague. That would be his economic suicide. It wasn't like he could mention this to the detective though.

There was silence between them. Detective Fakir seemed to be considering something as she looked into his eyes. Perhaps she wondered if there was another secret he was hiding from her. However, it was only for a short time.

"Will you take me to Chapel Park?" she then asked him.

Erol looked up, into her eyes, and nodded. It didn't seem like he had much of a choice.

***

Despite Erol's protests, the both of them had marched over to Chapel Park almost immediately. There was no time to waste lazying around. For all Annie knew, the murderer could be getting farther and farther away from them with every moment they wasted. Though the kebab-seller had suggested they went at night. Erol thought it was a way of getting proper details of the police, behind the watchful eyes of people. Perhaps Annie would have agreed if this case wasn't giving her enough stress already.

They arrived at the small terraced building. Annie was surprised to see that the lock had been broken, and so had Erol. The detective had one hand on her gun and looked around the place, but she found no one. Erol put his hand on the door and looked at her. She nodded.

He pushed at the door and it creaked open. They were

greeted first by a light cloud of dust, illuminated by the tiny rays of light from the cracks in the windows, evident that not only was the lock broken, the door itself was forced open from its hinges.

They both stood at the doorway. It was dark down the building. Only a small amount of light from the sun refracted through tiny cracks on the windows. Crystal had obviously made attempts to bolt her windows really tightly before leaving that night. In the rays of light, they could see dust particles performing the Brownian motion in the air.

Annie decided to completely release her gun which had still been strapped to her waist. With her left hand supporting the grip, she took a step forward, and then the next.

On the wall by the left was a toggle switch. She flicked it on, but the lights did not come on. She thought someone may have done this intentionally. That made her grip the gun tightly, hoping that someone would storm out from the dark and attack her. She wasn't very keen on dashing for the windows to lighten up the place. Who knew who could have been watching. It then occurred to her that she was with her phone.

She took it out and turned on the flash light. It may not be as bright as an electric bulb, but it was bright enough to show the way.

The hallway was reduced to rubble and rusty nails. Open wires dangle from the ceiling. A set of ladders rest against the wall next to an open pot of dried up paint. Detective Fakir moved quietly and slowly on the trash – Erol followed closely behind. She wondered how the woman had managed for a year in this dump without fixing it up herself.

The detective's torchlight led them to where she suspected might have been the living room. There was nothing in here but a few crushed beer cans on the floor and some shitty graffiti on the wall. Something nasty had definitely happened here, she thought. Maybe a bad gang had hosted themselves here?

They moved ahead. Erol followed closely behind. At one point, he snarled something hesitantly in Arabic, and the both of them had turned over soon to realize he's just walked into a cobweb. Annie was beginning to reconsider the decision to bring him along. But she couldn't sent him off. Especially since they hadn't covered the entire ground.

There was a wooden staircase leading up to the second floor. The torchlight revealed that it was dusty and there were no shoeprints. The stairs didn't look like it would be enough to hold their weight though.

But as they counted their way towards the staircase, Detective Fakir caught something in the light: footprints. They were travelling up the stairs. They had a unique crisscross pattern. But had she not looked at the stairs a while ago and had not seen footprints? Even Erol too was surprised. How come they suddenly became visible? They might probably need reminding that they were barely managing a phone's torchlight, and that they had surveyed the stairs from a distance. Or maybe they weren't alone in this dark building. Detective Fakir was not giving up, nonetheless. She had to satisfy her curiosity.

She took a quick photo of the stairs and the surrounding floor, before plunging ahead. The floorboards creaked under their weight as they made it up the stairs. Her right hand gripped the gun – the left hand only left its position when she was either supporting her stance or inspecting something.

Finally, they got to the room at the second floor. Detective Fakir pushed the door slowly and it creaked open. Erol peeped from behind.

There was a single light bulb hanging from the middle of the ceiling. The detective pulled a cord by the wall and the light flickered on. She then turned off her phone torchlight.

At a corner of the room, there was a flat, stained mattress with a small electric heater next to it. Clothes, shoes and underwear were strewn all over the floor, including the hoodie from the footage of the clothing store.

Erol stood at the center of the room whilst Detective Fakir wandered around, surveying the room. She went over to an upturned cardboard box that had been used as a table. A bunch of make-up was scattered on it alongside a portable flip mirror. She looked out the window, at the lamp post where she had seen Iman standing, and her gaze found the building the footage had come from, judging by its angle anyway.

"This was going to be the master suite," Erol commented, a bit proudly.

But there was no reply to that.

Annie shifted her attention to the mattress. On the floor beside it, there was the drug, paraphernalia – a pipe, foil, a lighter – some empty baggies. There was also a phone charger plugged into a socket on the wall, but it was not connected to a phone. Annie crouched down and let the wire run through her fingers. There were thoughts in her mind, but she had not settled on any of them yet. This entire place struck her as odd. This woman had had a life, however how bad it was. But this room would never feel her presence again, and those clothes would never cover her skin again, and perhaps no one would ever say her name again. That was the real death. To be forgotten. She wasn't going to let that happen.

As she examined the area, something sticking out from under the mattress caught her eyes. She stood up and lifted the mattress with her foot. It was a passport.

She crouched down and picked it up. On the cover, it read: *Union Européenne République Française.* She opened it. The data page gave the details of the woman – by the side was her passport photograph. Detective Fakir stared at it for a while. And then she looked around the room once again. It seemed like she had reached the end of her investigation in this building. It seemed like she had found what she was looking for.

She got to her feet and exhaled – for once, she lowered her gun and turned to Erol. He was still trying to get used to what he was seeing.

"Come on, let's go," she ordered.

CHAPTER THIRTEEN

Annie had thought discovering the victim's identity would be the key to finding out who the murderer was, but it appeared it had rather meant a ticket to National Television. The Dubai Police had, apparently, not liked the way they felt incompetent in the past few days, and they needed their first chance to assure the people the investigation was actively progressing. Annie also couldn't decline this interview, no thanks to her higher-ups. However, the entire thing was supposedly scripted and she wouldn't be put in an uncomfortable situation. Still, a streak of nervousness crept into her.

"A breakthrough on the seaside stabbing now as the victim has finally been identified as Yasmin Hojat, a French national of Lebanese descent. I am here with Detective Annie Fakir, who can perhaps explain why it took so long to find her in the first place?" the interviewer, a young European man (weirdly enough) with sleek brown hair and carefully shaped beards, said. Annie had learnt his name was Dylan Smith.

The camera shifted to Detective Fakir. She had a plain

expression on her face. Behind her were houses and people going about their duties while glancing the way of the interview. They'd thought it wise to host the interview on the streets in the area the murder had occurred.

"Well, that's hardly the question we need to be answering," she noted.

"It has to cross your mind that the killer could be miles away by now," the reporter cut in.

Annie frowned just so slightly. This wasn't how the interview had been scripted to progress. She quickly let words click in her mind. They were on Live television and she couldn't afford to make any mistakes. "The point is, we are one step closer to connecting the dots," Detective Fakir declared.

"And I believe the world would like to know more about Yasmin? I mean can you tell us what you know about her?" he asked, returning to the script.

"There isn't much at the moment. We are currently tracking down her family members whom we believe can hopefully shed some light on her story."

Dylan nodded gently at that. "Okay. But do you have anything with regard to potential suspects?" he said.

"Nothing concrete, but we're working on it."

"One last question, Detective Fakir. Do you have any comment on the recent speculation surrounding Robert Bloom?" he asked, once again completely ditching the script.

Annie nursed a measure of annoyance. "Like you said, it's pure speculation," she said to him. That rumour had been something Officer Hussain had mentioned a handful of times enough. But Annie was smart to understand they were based on an existing hate for the man. He was no one's favorite and every of his actions were overly criticized, including his involvement in that hotel that's being built. No one hated the hotel particularly, they just hated Robert Bloom's involvement. And the same thing now. No one knew he had anything to do with the murder. They simply liked to think he did.

And this reporter didn't seem like an exception. "Is it something you're going to pursue?" he asked.

"Well I have nothing else to say on the matter. Thank you," Annie said firmly and finally. She went behind the camera after she had said this. The reporter looked in her direction for a moment and then turned back at the camera.

The cameraman filmed from a yard or two in front of him and then faced the reporter once again with the camera. Annie stood off by the side.

"And that people, was the message from Annie Fakir, the detective in charge of the seaside murder case. It's been five days since the murder of Yasmin Hojat. One can only hope that soon, justice will prevail. Stay tuned as we continue to bring you updates regarding this particular case and more. I'm Dylan Smith for the Creek Observer online. Thank you. Bye for now," he said with a practiced smile.

"Aaaand CUT!" the cameraman yelled.

Dylan took out a bottle of water from the small bag that lay behind the camera all the while and drank from it. The cameraman began to pack up his gear.

"I think that was good, Annie," the reporter remarked.

"You threw me under the bus. What the hell was that?" Annie replied immediately. She wasn't on live TV anymore and could call him out on his shit.

"Hey, I'm just asking the same questions everybody else is asking," he said. Dylan shrugged and rolled his eyes. He opened the bottle and drank from it. "I have my honor as a reporter to find the truth. There are worried parents in this parts, Annie."

Annie frowned. "We're supposed to be on the same team, here. And you know I'm doing everything to figure all this out. Don't act like you care more about finding the murderer more than anyone else," she told him firmly before turning around.

"You want my advice?" Dylan called out behind her.

"Not particularly."

He let out a breath that made Annie believe he was wearing a smile. "Look into Bloom," he said.

"I'm not going to let my investigation be influenced by gossip, Dylan. People are only coming down on Bloom so he doesn't build his ostentatious hotel," she answered curtly, turning around lazily to see the reporter was all ready to move to their van.

"Still, it wouldn't hurt to pay him a visit. Clear his name and the pressure is off. Get a conviction and I might be able to report some good news for a change," Dylan said with a fatigue-ridden sigh. Then he made for the van and was off on his way.

Detective Fakir darkened the frown, as she mulled Dylan's words over.

Robert Bloom was one of the employees of a construction company. He had been arrested on Tuesday, 14th October, 2014 on bribery and tax evasion charges. Apparently, he had embezzled enough money to cause some affiliated businesses to go under. One of the businessmen had even killed himself a few years later when his business failed to kick back, as Annie had heard. The people had good reasons not to like Robert Bloom.

The man had been found guilty in court and was sentenced to six years in prison. Six months after the judgment was passed, his lawyer tried to appeal the sentence. This was in 2015. But it was overturned and that meant he had to serve out his entire sentence without parole until he was finally released in summer, 2020. He was easily recognized on the construction company's website in the group photo that was at the top of the homepage. In this photo, he could be seen looking right into the camera with an arrogant smirk across his face in his usual trucker cap.

Some people, apparently, his crimes couldn't be that forgotten, hence the hate towards him and all his businesses. Annie seriously doubted his hotel would be patronized if it was completed. *If.*

Whether Detective Fakir was going to investigate him or

not, she was not sure yet – she was more concerned with solving the mystery behind the death of Yasmin than devoting her time on Bloom at the moment.

Just as Annie was about to enter her car, her phone buzzed. A moment later, she was looking at Officer Kazeem's name on the screen of her phone.

"Please tell me you have good news," groaned Annie.

A smooth accent answered, "No. I checked the CCTV of the man's house to see if he caught whoever broke into Yasmin's house. They all came out blank. Every CCTV in a two-block radius was blank. I think they used some kind of *signal jammer* or something. Whoever this killer is, they're really cleaning up their tracks and they have the money or facilities to."

Annie cussed. "Alright. Thank you," she said.

"Do you really think they took Yasmin's phone?" Kazeem asked before Annie hung up.

"I think whoever killed her contacted her to meet at that point. If the phone hadn't been taken off her body, then it had been taken in the house. Probably disposed of by now," she explained her hypothesis. "Now we just have to find a match for that footprint and find that little girl."

"About the girl, we found someone matching her description yesterday night," Kazeem trailed on.

***

Detective Fakir approached the police station with urgency in her movements. The press still lingered around like flies around a rotten fruit. One of them whispered into the other's ear as the detective walked past them. She may have heard what was said, but she did not react to it. The whole interview with Dylan had certainly stirred something with the people. Annie simply frowned and continued on her journey up the steps. She almost didn't notice Officer Kazeem standing at one side as he had a hushed with a woman that looked like a reporter.

But then, her eyes shifted inadvertently to his direction. She stopped dead in her tracks. Kazeem took note of her just then and broke away from the woman. He changed course immediately and came to where Annie stood.

"*Ahlan*, Detective," he greeted. His dark eyes looked awfully dull and Annie blamed herself a little. He had been her unofficial partner in this case and he seemed to be quite overworked. The actual person assigned to her, Hussain, barely concerned himself with the case so Annie didn't really have a choice.

Annie nodded to his greeting. "Anything that concerns me?" she asked, nodding towards the woman who was already leaving the scene.

"Oh, no." Kazeem shook his head quickly. "That's just a reporter from Creek Observer who was covering a story on Robert Bloom. I did not offer any information to her though."

"Right." Annie turned towards the door of the Naif Police Station. "Is she in there?" she asked. Kazeem nodded. Then the both of them were soon striding into the station. They didn't have to walk long. The girl was sitting in the waiting room beside a man in a *kandora*, staring keenly at her hands.

"Her name is Iman Mehrabi. An officer was on patrol at the fair last night and he found that she matched the description you offered," explained Kazeem as he stood beside Annie. "He brought her in and she didn't make any resistance. She also hasn't spoken a word since then… or eaten anything."

Annie cussed. "She didn't spend the night in a cell, did she?" she asked.

Kazeem shook his head, momentarily stifling a yawn. "No. She wouldn't leave the waiting room. I think she's waiting for someone or looking for someone. Also, we didn't let this information get out since we aren't sure how much involvement she has with the case. So she's not considered a criminal or anything and can't be put in prison," he said. Annie sighed deeply and was striding forward when Kazeem stopped her and said, "You may need to work fast on the case though. I heard the sheikh himself might interfere if there isn't any progress soon."

Those words caused a streak of what could easily be summed up as fear run up Annie's spine. She shrugged it off quickly enough, nodded at Kazeem before walking towards the waiting room. The girl looked up now. There was a resignation in her demeanor. Like she'd given up on something. Annie swallowed.

"Hello! How are you doing?" she said in Arabic the moment she was within earshot. Kazeem had escorted the man in the kandora to his office to lodge a complaint. The girl didn't answer. She simply stared into Annie's eyes.

Then Annie repeated the same words in English, and it proved the same.

Like before, she simply looked deep into the eyes of the detective that had just greeted. Annie sighed. She considered her surroundings. There were police officers moving around and it was quite noisy, especially from the press just outside. They needed someplace more quiet.

Annie wasn't that good with children, her brother's twins were testament to that, so her voice was as formal as usual when she said, "Can you please come with me? There is something I need to ask you."

The girl did not say a word. But Annie desperately read her silence as agreement. She took her by the hand and they walked together. She had expected the little to put up some restraint, but nothing like that. Instead she followed her willingly. Again, Annie felt the wave of resignation and hopelessness. What exactly happened to this girl? What had happened to her in the past few days? This wasn't the same demeanor she had when Annie saw her skipping out of the cinema.

Annie was taking her straight to her office. She may not have been great with kids, but she knew the interrogation room was no place for a kid. She did notice that the girl kept looking around, observing the dull walls of the police station and the dim lighting. This one wasn't the way police stations were usually portrayed. In movies, they gave a sense of hope and determination, but here, it was a dark and gloomy thing that made one feel awfully exposed. The officers that moved around certainly didn't help.

While on their way to the office, Annie bumped into Officer Kazeem halfway through. He had been escorting the man that went into the office with him earlier.

"I'm sure your neighbor didn't deflate your tyres, Mr. Nair, but I will still look into it," he was explaining to the man who wore a very displeased look on his face. He paused before Annie.

"Please, take her to my office. I'll be with you soon," she told him. The girl herself didn't seem to mind the transition and obliged while Kazeem nodded. Annie herself then went back to the waiting room and towards the fridge to pick something. Then she headed back.

The door was quietly pushed open. She was greeted with the wooden table in her office and the assortment of files upon it. There were two wooden chairs upon which the girl sat upon one. The room was illuminated with dull grey lighting, and brightened up by Annie's very own terrible attempt at interior decoration. Eliza would shudder at this.

Officer Kazeem had already left, leaving the girl in the room. Annie found the girl propped herself up in her elbows on the table, her cheeks in the palms of her hands. There was no fear in her eyes as to what she might be getting into, just that resignation. However, it wasn't like things were looking that good for her. The girl may not have stolen anything from the clothing store as the attendant had complained the other day, but she had been caught kneeling beside the dead body and even made an attempt to touch her. If her explanation was not convincing enough, they would have to detain her, contrary to Kazeem's conclusion earlier.

After a short moment of observing the girl silently, Detective Fakir entered fully with two cans of orange juice, declaring her presence. She dropped one on the table in front of the girl and took the seat opposite her. But the girl showed not the slightest interest in the juice. She ignored it and looked down at the table.

"Your name is Iman, right?" Detective Fakir asked, trying to sound as friendly as she could.

Iman nodded.

Detective Fakir let out a smile that was intended to convince Iman that she was safe here.

"Nice to meet you, Iman. I'm Annie. I've been meaning to speak to you for a while now. I need you to understand that it's very important you tell me the truth today, okay?" she said very carefully. It was safe to conclude the girl understood English but she couldn't be sure just how much.

Iman nodded again.

"Good girl. You see, a friend of mine told me he saw you with the lady who died the other day. Is that true?" Detective Fakir observed as Iman's eyes dropped. She did not say a word or even attempt to nod this time. "You're not in trouble. I promise. I'm just trying to figure out what happened to her," Annie assured her.

"Was she my mum?" Iman asked.

"Oh no, dear, she wasn't your mum. The lady was from France. Are you from France?" Annie wore a gentle frown and tilted her head to one side.

For the first time, Iman made eye contact with the detective and shook her head. A short silence now existed between them. Detective Fakir wondered why she had asked if the lady was her mum. Had the person Kazeem speculated she was in search of her mother? She looked closely at her and noticed the bruise on her forehead that just escaped the cover of her beanie.

"That must hurt. How did you get it?" she inquired.

"I fell," Iman answered laconically.

Detective Fakir leaned forward. "Listen, Iman. I need to know if you saw something, maybe the night the lady was murdered…"

Iman put her brain to thought. Her face assumed a color as she tried to remember if she actually saw something. That was what Annie thought anyway. After a while, Iman ultimately shook her head again, causing Annie to shut her eyes for a slight second. "I was just looking for my mum," she said.

Annie uncorked the can and drank a little from it. It could have been a way of showing Iman that it was safe to drink hers.

That brought Iman's attention to hers. She glanced at it.

"Go on, it's yours," she encouraged her

But Iman refused. The detective still nurtured her patience. Although the questioning was not going as planned, she couldn't just dismiss Iman as a kook. She thought that perhaps she should take another direction.

"Why don't you tell me how you got here?" she asked.

"I ran away," Iman answered.

"From where or from whom?" asked Annie.

"A woman I lived with. Angie." Her voice was low while she whispered that detail.

"Were you no comfortable living with him?"

Iman shook her head. "I lived here with my mum and dad in London. We're from Iran. Then we were supposed to come here. My mum and I," she added. Her English was quite good.

"I see." Detective Fakir cocked a brow. She understood that she was loosening up now. She was hopeful that they would eventually come back to what happened to Yasmin. "What happened to your parents?"

"My dad died," Iman told his almost too sharply. Then she added very quietly, "They said he killed himself."

Detective Fakir gazed at her and the can of orange juice beside her briefly. She wished the interrogation took a bit different turn. If she dared applied pressure, Iman would get scared and that would not mean well for her investigation. She concluded it was best she did it her way.

"Why didn't your mum look after you then?"

Iman seemed to be a little reluctant to answer that, but she did anyway, with the hope that Detective Fakir would help her, maybe. "There was an accident. I don't know what happened. We were in a train coming to Deira when it happened. I woke up on the floor and the train was gone. Angie took me in before I came here," she explained.

"So you came back to look for her?"

"Yes. Will you help me?" a plea settled in her voice.

Detective Fakir took a deep breath, taking it all in. She had clearly gotten more than she had bargained for. A little girl looking for her mother whom people say is crazy? It was a lot to take in. If she was going to figure this out though, she might have to start from the train accident Iman mentioned. But this wasn't a priority for Annie right now. She could have someone else do that though.

However, she thought that it would not be wise to allow Iman return to the streets. She would be a terrible person if she threw her out after the interrogation. Iman looked visibly unkempt and emaciated – that should count for something.

There was nothing more to ask her, Detective Fakir thought. There would have to be another attempt before she questioned her further on the murder of Yasmin Hojat. And so she thought it was better she took her to her own house once she was done with today's work. With that, she lodged Iman in her office while she worked. Her share of the drink on the table remained unopened

CHAPTER FOURTEEN

Annie had taken a break from work, entrusting Iman with Kazeem while she went ahead to make room for Iman at home, and get Eliza onboard with the whole arrangement. It was the only thing she could do really given her lack of any further clues. This was simply a very needed distraction.

And in her living room, she laid on the sofa. Her eyes were closed as she rested her head on Eliza's lap. They were having some cuddly time. Soft music played in the background and the other woman smelt like sweet perfumes. Eliza ran her fingers through Annie's hair. That was the charm that kept her eyes closed and brought out the goose bumps on her skin. But then she stopped to pick up her phone.

"Please don't stop. I might actually be able to relax enough before going back to the station," Annie said – she sounded like a kid begging to be cuddled to bed. And she didn't mind it. She deserved these moments, especially after cleaning up the room reserved for Iman.

Eliza continued to stroke Annie's hair and chuckled softly. "I used to love it when my mum did this to me as a kid," Eliza recalled as her svelte fingers formed a trail along Annie's hair. Annie took a deep, relaxing breath and shuffled on the chair. "Can I tell you something?" she asked.

"Do you have another street child you want to bring in?" Eliza asked, laughing at her own joke. Then she answered more curtly, "Always."

"The other night in the restaurant, there was a guy…"

"On the table that wouldn't shut up the entire time," Eliza cut in – she already knew.

"Mm-hmm," Annie agreed.

Eliza looked at her face – from her smooth forehead and the space between her eyes and then her nose that slanted prominently. "Don't tell me he was your ex," she alleged.

Annie sat up, a wry smile forming on her face. The sleep appeared to have left her eyes. The conversation was starting to get serious and needed urgent attention.

"Wait, really?" Eliza asked.

Annie buried her head between her knees.

"That's your type?" Eliza added.

The space between her brows had creased in disappointment. Her lips seemed to be trembling.

"I don't know – he was fun, I guess," Annie replie

shrugging a little. "Fun?"

"Yeah."

Eliza stopped stroking Annie's hair. The disappointment she felt had finally reached its peak. She still couldn't believe Annie would find such a guy attractive or fun to be with. Eliza was a judgmental one and quite easy to read. Annie knew she thought him arrogant and foolish.

"What?" Annie retorted.

The smile on her face disappeared. Now it dawned on her how serious Eliza took the issue. There was an awkward silence between them now. But it lasted for a few seconds. It was broken when Annie's phone chimed on the stool.

She picked up the phone. *Hello... ... No, no... Sure...*

Even as Annie continued speaking with Hussain on the other line, she knew Eliza was still upset about the situation. Was it jealousy? Or was it that she thought that the guy was not worthy of Annie? Or was it that Annie condescended so low to date such a loud guy? Whatever her reason was, her conclusion was that Annie disappointed her, it seemed.

Eliza sighed and filled up her wine glass as Annie sat up quickly and said, "I have to go now. I'll be back soon enough and with the girl." Then she added for good measures. "I love you, okay?"

"I love you too," said Eliza, finally smiling.

***

Detective Fakir was standing in the middle of a cozy bedroom. There was a large double bed in the room and dried flowers on the dresser. The room was tidy and smelt as though it had an open source of chocolate somewhere. Iman stood by the door.

"This is where you will be sleeping henceforth. It's only the spare room but I'm pretty sure it is better than the boat you mentioned," Annie explained. Her hair had fallen loose from its bun and now fell down the side of her face like a storm of raven feathers.

Iman stepped inside, her eyes scanning the room, struggling to contain the excitement she felt. She liked it here. She preferred it to Erol's place, even though she never saw it. It was obvious she did not trust Erol as much as to live with him. Or maybe it was simply her experience with Angie, the woman she'd lived with for the better part of the previous year. With the detective, it felt different. And here, it was best to live with a woman that would represent as her mother, at least for now, till she found her own.

"So make yourself comfortable okay? I'll be with you soon," Detective Fakir said, motioning her hand towards the room.

"Thank you," Iman appreciated – there was a rhapsody of excitement in her voice. It was lighter than it had ever been in a long time.

"You're welcome," Detective Fakir responded and left the room.

Iman explored every part of it; from the wardrobe to the bathroom and back to the room. She pressed her fist on the bed and then sat on it. Soft and comfortable it felt. She had not lain on something as soft as this in a long time. She had been lying on woods and other hard surfaces. Now she finally got a chance at comfort again. She gently lay on the bed.

And truthfully, she thought she could lay upon it forever.

Later at night, Annie, Iman and Eliza sat around the table eating takeaway pizzas. Eliza and Annie exchanged glances as Iman grabbed another slice from the box and took a huge bite, stuffing it down her throat. If only they could understand how she had been surviving all this while. If only they knew the contents of her menu, they would understand why she felt like shoving it all down her throat.

"So, I told my niece about Iman and she was kind enough to lend out some of her clothes," Eliza told them. Then she turned to Iman, her strange eyes stirring with an emotion Iman couldn't quite identify. "Do you wanna try them on after dinner?" she asked.

Iman nodded politely. But even so, her disinterest could be seen in her eyes. And living with a detective and her friend who had copied some of her sleuthing skills, it was difficult to hide feelings.

"Oh, you don't have to. It was just an idea," Eliza tried to bail herself.

"Is there something else you feel like doing?" Annie asked.

They were both looking at Iman now like parents who were trying to understand their daughter. That sort of felt awkward. But if that question was for real, she had a lot to do. She could start by watching the TV. Ever since her iPad's charger had been misplaced (it was due anyway) she had not been watching movies and that had worsened the boredom and depressive nights… and the nightmares.

Iman loved the life the detective had offered her, but she had not lost the will to look for her mother, nonetheless. A little break, however, wouldn't hurt much. So she didn't hesitate or hold back in requesting for what she needed. It wouldn't hurt anyone to.

Soon afterwards, she was sitting between Annie and Eliza on the couch, watching the TV with the lights off – loud intense horror music blasting off the speakers. The fear and horror were comforting to Iman at this point.

"Don't go in there! Oh my god, I can't watch this," Eliza yelled and covered her eyes.

Iman turned to Annie and chuckle lightly. She might be the youngest amongst them, but in horror movies, she was older than the both of them combined. And Annie wasted no time to find out.

"Are you sure you've seen this movie before?" Annie asked Iman.

Iman nodded enthusiastically and turned her attention back to the movie. Annie forced an uncomfortable smile. She had voiced out how surprising it was that Iman could comfortably watch such a horrifying movie earlier. She's also mentioned how it was strange and quite disturbing. Iman only wore a tight smile then though.

How was she to explain to the detective that she watched all these scary things to distract herself from the things she considered truly scary. Her memories. Most of the time, she forgot a lot of the dark streaks of her memories when she watched these things and she liked it that way. She wanted to forget about the man that had visited her and her mother in London to inform them of her father's passing. She wanted to forget the violent separation from her mother two years ago. And her freshest memory; the lifeless woman with the empty eyes staring into the sky that looked a lot like her mother.

And she did forget them all right here.

When the movie ended, it was time to retire to bed. Iman was used to sleeping late at night because she stayed awake to watch movies, but she was pretty exhausted. And with the promise of a comfortable bed this night, it would be an effortless journey to dreamland.

She had wasted no time diving on the bed after she had bid goodnight to the ladies. Now she lay on the bed, fast asleep.

***

Annie watched her from the doorway as she coiled up on the bed. She looked like a pitiful lamb. All she's needed was to wash up and get into clean clothes and she's completely transformed.

But there was one other thing tugging at Annie's heartstrings. How would she find Iman's mother? Having been told that the poor girl was looking for her mother, she felt obligated to help her find her. But Iman had not provided any meaningful clue as to where to look. She couldn't just be wandering about the street. Though she's mentioned this to Kazeem and he'd agreed to look into any major train wrecks in the past five years, Annie still felt it would take some time. She would also have to first finish with the urgent case she had at hand before going ahead to look for Iman's mother. Yasmin Hojat's murderer still ran freely and that scared her more than she would like to admit. The case was drawing too much attention than they needed.

With that thought now taking root in her head, she turned off the lights and closed the door quietly behind her.

Eliza was waiting when Annie came back and soon they were both in the kitchen washing the dishes.

"All I'm saying is that you surprise me sometimes. You never let me stay the night," Eliza complained.

"What was I supposed to do?" Annie asked.

She handed Eliza the plate she had just washed and she rinsed it.

"Hey, relax. I'm kidding okay. I can't imagine how it was out there all night," Eliza brought the emotions to control immediately.

And then she dropped her towel and took Annie by the hips. Across her face was a coquettish smile – she bit down on her bottom lip.

"You were so cute tonight," she lauded Annie, pulling her even closer that their bodies had no space left between them.

And soon, their lips locked in a kiss. It lasted for a while and then Eliza pulled out. "I think you'd make a super cool mum," she whispered softly, licking Annie's ear.

That would have taken them both to a height of ecstasy. But Annie scoffed and broke free. She went back to the dishes.

"What? I'm serious. Do you ever think about having kids?" Eliza questioned picking up the towel and tying it around her chest.

"I dunno. Sometimes. Why, do you?" Annie intoned.

"Of course I do."

Annie scrubbed the plate so hard it seemed as though something was stuck on it. Eliza smirked at her attempt to distract them from the conversation.

"You should let child protection services know," Eliza suggested.

"I need more time. There's something she's not telling me, plus she won't be considered as a high risk case" Annie replied.

Eliza took the plate that had just been washed and rinsed it and then placed it gently in the rack.

"Won't you get into trouble? I don't think your position as a detective exempt you from the punishment involved you know."

Annie stopped washing the plate she was holding now.

"Isn't it strange that she wanted to watch a scary movie? I mean a scary movie in the dead of the night. It's quite unsettling if you ask me," she noted.

"Oh that! I didn't really think about it," Eliza replied.

Annie was now washing the last plate in the sink. In her head were thoughts about Iman's strange behavior. She couldn't stop remembering the smirk on her face when all the while the movie was going on. Not even a frown – not a sign at all that she was scared, especially with all the gory scenes; swords slicing through flesh, chainsaw drilling through someone's skull and knife cutting out the flesh on the face of someone, leaving them bleeding horribly – neither of these was scary to an 11-year-old girl. Annie was disturbed. She thought Iman's mind must have been messed up really badly to be comfortable with all that. Little wonder she was able to live in a boat for weeks.

After her time with Annie, Eliza was ready to leave. She walked through the front door. Annie stood by it. They'd decided Eliza wouldn't stay after all. Eliza had an early morning at work too and Annie already had instructions from Hussain to look into Bloom finally.

"See you tomorrow?" Eliza asked. It was meant to be rhetoric, but Annie answered.

"I hope so but…"

"I understand," Eliza cut in.

She pushed closer and they kissed. Eliza then pulled Annie to herself – they were just as close as they were back in the kitchen. Their eyes were closed as their lips locked into a torrid snog. It was meant to be the final kiss till they saw each other again, until suddenly, they heard the saw a flash and heard the camera shutter.

They pulled out quickly and turned around to find a photographer across the walkway. He was still in position, pointing the camera at them. Annie quickly hid her face. She panicked and ran inside the house, slamming the door shut behind her and abandoning Eliza.

Still, she felt her body move towards the window and she realized Eliza had not been as bothered as she was. Eliza scoffed and turned to the photographer, who took another picture, this time, a much clearer one of her face.

"Fuck off," Eliza spat, motioning for her shoe.

The photographer was clearly not moved by the other lady's threat. He took a couple more of the pictures before finally heading away in the opposite direction. This time because Eliza actually moved closer to him with the shoe raised in the air.

Once he was gone, Eliza looked towards the window and caught Annie's gaze. She offered a smile. Annie felt the tension within her stir once more and shut the curtains, cutting her view off her lover.

She sat on the sofa and stared at the wall for several minutes.

***

The Man observed the newly-printed pictures with a lewd smile before placing them back in the folder he had in his hand. Then he tossed the file aside and strolled out of the room into the living room where his wife stayed glued to the TV.

"Honey, I told you not to spend your time watching this. There are no good news out there," he said.

His wife was still wearing the same expensive abaya she's been wearing earlier today which almost completely covered up the bump that had formed in her stomach. Her long eyelashes fluttered wildly as she turned towards him. "They still haven't found the one who murdered her," she said, tension rising in her voice.

The Man sat beside her and wrapped his arms around her lovingly, gently trailing a hand over her belly. In another memory, it wasn't her stomach he was touching. It was someone else's. He shook his head and smiled. "They'll catch him soon enough," he said with so much certainty. "Don't worry, you're safe. I'll make sure of that."

And he had made sure of that. He was safe.

CHAPTER FIFTEEN

"You'll call me Angie," the tall woman said to Iman. She was wearing an abaya and her hands were inked with henna. Her heavily lined eyes looked down on the girl who's just blinked awake on the mat, and her red lips were curled into a snarl.

Iman blinked and stirred on the raffia mat she's found herself on. Her movement drew her attention to the bandages and plasters all over her body, and the pain the wounds underneath all those dressing brought. "Where am I?" she managed to ask.

Angie rolled her eyes. "I found you and treated you with my money. You could at least appreciate that first," she all but spat in Iman's face. Then she proceeded to say something vile in Arabic.

"I'm sorry. Thank you," came Iman's broken voice. Her attention snapped then. "Mum!" She looked at the woman in the abaya and asked, "Do you know what happened to my mother?"

Iman felt the slap before she saw it. There had been a bruise on her cheek already and this impact simply caused Iman to wince terribly.

Her eyes reddened and she tried to fight back a sob. There wasn't a lot of progress with that.

The tall woman, Angie, crouched and sat on the mat and then wrapped her arms around Iman tenderly, almost like a mother. The action confused her greatly but she found herself sinking into the feeling. It was comfortable, in the least. She felt the woman's breath at her ear as she said, "Your mother is dead." The woman's touch suddenly felt cold and her voice like razors into Iman's heart. Imam was too shocked to move. "That's right. Your train was attacked by bandits. Everyone died, except you because you crashed into the window and fell on the floor. You're all alone in the world ..." Then her voice warmed as she added, "But you have me. Angie."

Angie let go of Iman and withdrew her face. She was a beautiful woman but those eyes of hers housed something very ugly. She gently used her thumb to wipe a tear from Iman's face.

"But you will be fine. For every horror you experience," continued Angie, allowing her finger trail down to the point she'd hit Iman, "you have to remember there is always something worse. There is always something scarier in this world for people like us, and knowing that will help you forget everything you experience and set you goal on what you really want. Do you understand?"

Iman sniffed and nodded.

"So don't cry, my little djinn. You have me. Angie. So, tell me, what do you really want?"

Her response had been silent. Buts he knew on that day as she laid on that mat in the deadbeat house she would later share with Angie for a year, she was going to go to Deira as her mother had mentioned, and she would find her mother waiting for her there.

And to make her mind forget all the hurt and the pain and her fears – most of which she would experience at Angie's hands – she found something scarier to help with that.

***

Maybe it was about time she faced those fears.

Buried amongst the sheets, Iman shuffled around the bed. It had been a wonderful night – quite a long time since she had had such a beautiful sleep. Her body was neither achy nor weak. The room smelt so nice and she loved it. It felt like she had finally been reunited with her mother and that everything had come to back to normalcy.

It was time to get off the bed. She slouched about a little longer before gliding off. She yawned deeply and stretched stiffly like a hard rubber – her skin nearly snapped. And then she shuffled out of the room. She was wearing nicely-fit pajamas with the detective had helped procure – one of the things that reminded her of what used to be.

With her tousled hair, she walked slowly down the stairs, listening for any sound of life, but it was all quiet. She kept looking around and walking until she found herself in the kitchen.

Being in here, and given the absence of the detective anywhere, there was only part of it she could go; the fridge. She went closer and opened it. It was stocked with all kinds of food. But her eyes found a can of orange juice, similar to what she had rejected yesterday. She thought it was time she did justice to it – after all, she had gotten used to Annie already. Maybe too quickly.

Iman admitted though, when the police had taken her that day at the fair, she had thought that was the end. She would be shipped back off to Angie if she was lucky. But she wasn't always lucky, was she? So she knew she would end up in prison. She had been sure of that. Now, she wasn't very sure of anything anymore. With a content smile, she reached forth and took the can and then closed the fridge. The drink fizzled in the can as she squeezed the cover. She poured down some of it and left the kitchen. She was feeling at home indeed, just like Annie had permitted.

She made her way down the hallway. There was a bookshelf by the side. Bearing the can of drink in one hand, she browsed the shelf. One of the large books caught her eye. But it wasn't a book – it was a photo album.

She sat on the ground and flipped through the pages. But then a page caught her attention. In the photo inset in a larger frame, she saw a teenage Annie. She sat at a dinner table with a frown on her face as if she was forced to take that photo and with a scarf covering her head unlike she was now. The disinterest in her face could easily be seen. She was playing a retro Gameboy. Also in the photo were her parents. Her father wore a shirt and tie and his lips pouted as he tried to blow out the candles on the birthday cake in front of them. Her mother, wearing a traditional Shari, stood behind him, with her hands together. Iman could tell she had been clapping them when the photo was taken. There was another older boy somewhere in the background, almost cut out from the picture.

Iman turned a couple more pages and stopped at another inset photo. In it was Annie in her 20s. Judging from the background, Iman could tell that she was at a house party, posing with a couple of friends. She was holding a beer in one hand and her lips pressing on those of a boy.

At that, Iman frowned, a little confused. But then she moved over to the next page. In this photo, Annie was dressed in full police uniform; the olive green clothing that had been a flag that symbolized fleeing to Iman. The photo was taken outside the Naif Police Station, it appeared. She held up a certificate with a wide smile on her face.

Iman lingered on the photo. She was pleased with the smile, the glory the photo showed. It was great for some-one to be able to finally achieve their dreams after going through many challenges. The smile would be just as bright as that in the photo.

Knock! Knock!!

Instantly, another image flashed into Iman's mind. It was the direct opposite of this, lacking the glory and the hap-piness. It was the face of a very displeased man whose eyes met with hers.

Gasping, Iman backed away from the photo album. Just as quickly as it had come, the flash vanished. The knock came again and she turned slowly towards the direction of the door.

"Iman, it's me, Eliza. Annie told me to check up on you because she had to go somewhere," a familiar voice called out from outside. That was when Iman released a sigh and turned back to Detective Fakir's smiling face in the photo album. Only this time, she saw Annie standing in place of the dead woman in her nightmares.

***

It was still quite early in the morning and Annie wasn't supposed to be here yet. But every time she sat in that house, she kept remembering that click and the flash that followed. Someone somewhere had that picture of her with Eliza. And she needed a good distraction not to dwell on that. Hence her little morning expenditure.

She was in a construction yard. A crappy, run-down old caravan was at the middle of the desolate yard. She approached the door cautiously, gripping tight to her gun. She knocked, but there was silence. It didn't seem like anyone had been here in a long while.

However, she noticed the lock at the gate of the yard had been broken. She opened it a crack and peered inside curiously. "Mister Bloom?" she called, her voice echoed down the construction yard.

There was movement inside; a thud and a clang. The detective stepped backwards.

Eventually, the door of the caravan flung open to reveal Robert Bloom, looking worse for wear; eyes red, sweaty and wearing a vest.

Annie straightened as she took in his sight. "Mister Bloom, I am…" she began.

"I know who you are," he snapped.

Annie went silent at once. They both shared awkward looks. And then the European man turned and walked back inside, leaving the door open.

The detective followed, taking it as an invitation.

Inside the caravan was a total dump – a duvet and a pillow were crumpled on a withered brown couch. There was an empty whiskey bottle on the floor and the tiny sink was full of dirty dishes.

Robert Bloom put his trucker cap on and poured himself a glass of water. He watched the detective cautiously as she looked around inquisitively.

"I was wondering when you'd show up," he finally spoke. His flaky voice caught Detective Fakir's attention. She had been engrossed for a moment with her surroundings, not sure if she did well to hide the pity she felt.

"I just wanted to talk – off the record," she replied.

Bloom was silent. And then as if he just remembered that he poured himself a glass of water a moment ago, he reached for it and gulped down some quantity, smacking his lips lightly as though the water was bitter. Detective Fakir managed to hide the disgust she felt now.

"All I'm trying to do is get my life back together, and they're coming after me like a swarm of vultures," Robert said, trailing his hand through her brown hair. He gulped down half the glass of water. It was like the more words he spoke, the thirstier he became.

"How did you get the deal for the hotel?" Annie asked. If people hated him well enough, why give him jobs?

"How do you think I did? Connections, of course. People seem to forget that I built half this town." There was an edge of annoyance in his voice. "Little fishing Dubai settlement transformed into this glorious place where people from all over the world can come and be a part of." He sighed.

Annie shrugged. "Then you embezzled enough money to put a lot of your clients out of business," she added.

Bloom got up from the scrap of steel he had been sitting on and walked past the detective. He went and plonked down on the couch – his butt seemed to have been hurting all the while he was sitting on the scrap. Annie all the while, picking out every slight changes in his demeanor and his behavior.

"Listen, I know I'm a money-grabbing scumbag but I wouldn't kill some girl for a fucking PR stunt. I wouldn't kill anyone, full stop," he said to her.

Silence!

"Tell me the truth, did you know Yasmin?" Detective Fakir broke it.

"I used her a few times since I got out. Prison was rough, you know."

"I get it. But have you any idea who might have wanted to hurt her? I mean someone capable of taking her life?" Annie asked. "And where were you between the hours of 10pm and dawn on the night she was murdered?"

Bloom sniggered. "Are you sure this is off the record?" he asked.

"Mm-hmm."

"Well, seeing as I was busy with the few people that would still work with me the whole day, I was probably buried at the bottom of a bottle that night," he told her flatly, hid demeanor reeking with nonchalance. "As for who could have hurt Crystal… or Yasmin, not a clue. Excuse me. I need to use the toilet."

Robert Bloom the got up and was quick to shut himself in the small cubicle built into the caravan, leaving the detective to peruse his quarters. She walked around taking in every detail. Bloom's flow could be heard spattering in the water.

Detective Fakir wandered into the kitchen area, grimacing at the sink full of dirty dishes. Then, she spotted a set of knives in a wooden block. She frowned. Either she was hallucinating or they had the same deep red handle as the murder weapon.

From their positions, Detective Fakir observed that one of them was missing. She slid out one of them, a shiver running through her entire body. At this time, she could no longer hear the flow, but the sound of the toilet flushing. She quickly slid the knife back in its place and left the kitchen. Bloom was coming out of the toilet at the same time, zipping up his trouser.

Their eyes locked in – thoughts finding their way into their minds.

"What?" Bloom asked, raising a brow. He seemed to have no idea what Detective Fakir had been up to.

And that was the beginning of his problems.

CHAPTER SIXTEEN

Erol was supposed to be here. He just didn't know it yet. He strolled lazily through his restaurant to the meat truck that had just come to a stop. His friend, Ahmed, had already highlighted and was now opening the booth of the truck.

"You're late today," said Erol flatly. It was already ten in the morning, and even Erol had woken up early today.

Ahmed shrugged. "Married life isn't full of advantages alone," he said, shrugging. His eyes were was dullest thing Erol had seen all day and he looked like he wanted to get away as soon as possible.

"Hmm. How's Nafisat doing? I don't think she'll be very calm with a murderer on the loose. Hell, none of the women in these parts are calm," he said.

The meat seller paused in his attempt to pick up a cartoon of meat and looked at Erol with a frown. "You don't know? They already arrested the killer today. It should be on Creek Observer right now, even," he said.

Frowning, Erol slipped quickly into his restaurant. He'd already fixed the plug but now watched it far less since a certain someone didn't show up. He reached for the remote quickly and switched it on.

A news report came on screen. Outside the police station, Robert Bloom was being escorted up the steps by a policeman. He was in handcuffs. Beside him was his lawyer – a man in his 40s, bald and wearing a cheap suit. A few members of the press crowded around pointing microphones in his face. The paparazzi were there to make sure no scene was missed in the parade.

"Disgraced local businessman Robert Bloom was arrested again earlier today, only months after his release from prison, this time, under suspicion of murdering French Lebanese sex worker, Yasmin Hojat." A wave of fury charged up through Erol. All the while and it had been Robert who'd done it? "It came after investigators found links to the murder weapon at his residence on the outskirts of town. Deira Police have been faced with mounting pressure to solve this case. And it seems like they have finally found the killer," the reporter of Creek Observer who Erol knew as Dylan Smith said.

As Robert Bloom reached the top of the steps, members of the press threw a battery of questions at him.

Mister Bloom, did you kill her?

Was the baby yours?

Is there anyone else involved?"

Robert Bloom decided to stop then, to the protest of the officer leading him, and address the small crowd of people below. "All I know is that I'm an innocent man. Innocent! That's all I have to say," he declared to them all, almost roaring.

That was certainly not enough for the members of the press. They wanted more. Even when he had reached upstairs, they still struggled to reach him. But the officers downstairs held them back as Robert Bloom went into the Naif Police Station, flanked by his lawyer.

"Stay tuned for more updates right here on Creek Observer dot com" Dylan concluded before the channel brought up another clip.

"And the neighborhood is safe once again," a voice said beside Erol. Ahmed dropped the carton of meat on the counter as Erol turned around. The meat seller still seemed tired and dull but he wore a small smile now.

Erol let out a breath. "I just can't believe it was him," he confessed. "But why would he do it? Having a baby isn't something to kill for, is it?"

"How should I know?" shrugged Ahmed. He stretched forth his hand. "Now, pay up. And go get yourself a wife. Maybe the sheikh's daughter. I hear she's pretty."

Those words caused Erol to smile slightly and reach into the pockets of his white robe. "Right."

***

And now, Bloom was in the interrogation room. It would have been a thorough grilling was his lawyer not there to defend his rights.

He sat next to his lawyer with a displeased frown. Annie couldn't be sure if he was frowning because of the situation he was currently in or because he'd been refused a stick of cigarette when he'd asked for one earlier. Annie couldn't have given him the cigarette even if she wanted to anyway. This was a police station and that was the last thing allowed around here.

His lawyer sat rather too comfortably for one representing a murder suspect. He had his left leg crossed over his right, tapping on his phone. Officer Hussain and Officer Kazeem had just walked in and stood behind where Annie herself sat in the chair opposite them. She leaned forward on the table, staring down at Bloom. She wore an expression different from that Bloom saw when she visited his place. This one was more intense − more tyrannical, and she wanted him to feel it.

"I can't explain it, that's the fucking problem. I… I've had the set for years. They were a gift. I didn't even notice it was missing," Robert began to protest as wildly as he had when Annie arrested him back at the construction yard.

"The knife is hardly concrete evidence without any prints. It could've come from any one of a thousand sets," his lawyer defended, still tapping on his phone and not looking up as he talked. "It's a little coincidental though, don't you think?" he asked. He lifted his gaze. "Especially with the number of people that want my client taken away."

Everyone in the room was quiet as Annie and the layer

held each other's gazes as though they were in the middle of a staring contest.

"The last thing I want is to go back to jail," Bloom resumed, causing both of them to break the gaze and turn over to him.

"My client's home was broken into," his lawyer revealed. "The door was forced open. You could see for yourself. The knife was clearly stolen. I'd say he's the victim here and you should be protecting him not the other way around."

"And you didn't think to report this?" Annie questioned Bloom.

The lawyer put his hand on Bloom's shoulder and whispered something into his ear, not minding that Detective Fakir and two other officers were there, watching them. Bloom nodded to whatever he had told him.

"I've been drinking a lot, I mentioned. I didn't realize," he said.

Detective Fakir sighed. It was obvious that he had said what his lawyer had just whispered into his ear. But as she did not hear what was whispered, she did not count on that. Moreover, remembering the state of the man's apartment, there was no doubt of the drinking part.

"Unless you have any evidence that connects my client directly to the crime, we have nothing else to say. You've got precisely," the lawyer looked at his watch in well-composed movements, "twenty-two hours and fifteen – wait – fourteen minutes before I walk Mister Bloom right out of these doors."

His mouth creased into a smirk Detective Fakir wished she could slap off his face. She was getting infuriated now by the lawyer's show of pomposity. Because there were no fingerprints found on the murder weapon, he was convinced that there was no way the detective could prove that his client was the killer. And that got Detective Fakir irritated.

Now she locked eyes with Bloom. Her eyes burnt with fury – they were deep and consuming. She could see the look in Bloom's eyes. The fear in them was real and strong. She had managed to imbue fear in them. But she was not to revel in that yet – instead, she was to capitalize on it. If Bloom was guilty, then she had to go extra miles to prove it.

***

Night came over the Dubai Creek. Iman was in her room preening herself in the mirror. She was dressed in a white flowery dress – one of Eliza's niece's. She was not sure of the image she saw in the mirror – she was not comfortable either – she kept fiddling with its frills. The whole day, she had allowed her curiosity spend itself in every part of the house along with Eliza sometimes, though the woman had mostly been busy in from t of her computer. And when Iman had gotten tired of looking around, she brought herself on the chair, watched movies and slept, woke up and continued the movie from where she stopped, while eating anytime she found herself awake. It was a lazy routine but she liked it... at least, for now.

Her mind had still been bugged terribly by visions and memories she kept trying to push out.

While she adjusted the dress in her room, she heard voices downstairs – those of Annie and Eliza. They seemed to be having a misunderstanding. Curious, she cascaded down the stairs. But she needed not descend the whole flight of stairs – she could hear them clearly from her position halfway down.

In the kitchen, Eliza was sitting on the counter as Annie paced around the kitchen – her face appeared to not have witnessed laughter the whole day.

"I just came over to see how you were doing, Annie. I was here with Iman most of the day but… I'm worried about you," Eliza said – it was with a calm tone.

Iman couldn't help but notice Annie looked like and enraged Angie. It was like those times something went wrong in one of Angie's heists and the both of them, including a boy that had stayed with them at one point, had to pack and move to another town. It was more like a transferred aggression. Iman saw right through that. It didn't seem like Eliza did though.

"And I am telling you I need some space," Annie hissed.

"Because of what happened last night?"

"Maybe."

Eliza grabbed tufts of her hair in frustration. Iman frowned and wondered what exactly had happened the previous night after she'd gone to bed. She only knew that whatever it was that had happened had been the reason the detective was gone by morning, and the reason for this fight… apparently.

"Oh my goodness!" Eliza exclaimed.

"I have a murder investigation on my hands, Eliza. The last thing I need is people talking about us," Annie explained further, still holding that aggression in her tone.

"Who gives a fuck?"

"What?"

Iman was still hanging halfway down the stairs and listening to this squabble. She hated to see them this way. The argument… it reminded her awfully of something similar she'd encountered recently. Something--

"I mean, seriously? You need to get over yourself," Eliza advised.

Annie paused and scoffed. "Get over myself? That's real supportive, thank you," she said sarcastically.

"Do you really think people give a shit about your private life?"

"Hell yes they do! They look to me for answers! My mum. My dad. This entire fucking town. I need to be strong. And by the way, this thing between us is not allowed in this part of the world. I have mentioned it to you over and over again, yet you chose not to understand," she snapped.

"There's nothing stronger than being honest about whom you are," Eliza pointed out – neglecting the last part of Annie's statement. Her tone softened along with her expression as she said, "But do you even know who you are?"

"You know nothing about who I am! So don't even act like you do."

There was silence now. Eliza took a breath and dropped from the counter she had been sitting on. She seemed tired of the arguments already.

"I think I have to go n…" she announced.

"Yeah, I think you should," Annie replied even before she finished her words.

Eliza walked towards the door, but stopped by it. "I know it's scary…" she began.

"Please, Eliza."

That glued her tongue to her palate. "Tell Iman I said *bye*." She took one final glance at Annie and walked out left.

Iman heard footsteps. Someone was coming. She crouched on. She could see Eliza exit out the front door and wait for a cab by the roadside. And that meant Annie could be out of the kitchen anytime. She crept back up the flight of stairs and into her room.

That was when it happened. She didn't know what exactly had made it happen. Perhaps it was just due, like a stretched rubber snapping from the pressure. Or maybe it was something she'd heard or felt recently. Iman didn't know the reason, and truthfully, it was far from the last thing on her mind. Because right now, all the memories and pain and fears she'd been taught to bury up suddenly resurfaced.

And when the face of a particular man flashed in her vision this time, she held on to it.

***

It had been a bad day for Annie, but she was at the end of it. There had just been too much. Arresting Robert Bloom without getting any substantial evidence has made her higher-ups warn her that she had better not be wrong. It would be really bad on the Dubai Police Force. There had even been talks on just ditching the search for an evidence and let Bloom go down for it. No one would miss him anyway. And as if that hadn't been enough, Annie had received a call from her mother too. At first, she had thought the pictures had been sent to her parents and she was in for some trouble. Her relieve and displeasure had been fairly evident when she discovered her mother had called only because she'd seen Annie's press interview and noticed she wasn't wearing a scarf. And now, there was thing with Eliza. Pretty much the definition of a bad day.

The most Annie could do now was fix herself with something that would occupy her boiling temperament. And yes, she did find something to do just that.

She had her laptop set up on the dining room table. She adjusted her glasses, clicking from one part of the laptop to another. Beside the laptop was a steaming cup of tea to appeal to her senses.

On the laptop screen was the CCTV footage of a man breaking into a familiar place; Bloom's Construction Yard. It was the day of the murder, and the time at the corner of the footage read 04:16pm. He wore a balaclava and gloves as he worked on the front door with a crow bar. Bloom might have lived in a dump but his neighbor didn't. Unfortunately, this was proof of Bloom's innocence just like the man's lawyer had said in the mail this clip was attached to. Annie could just imagine this person breaking into Yasmin's Hojat's house at 54 Chapel Park. Though it was weird the bastard didn't bring his signal jammer this time.

Annie watched on, her head in her hands and trying not to let out a loud cuss. But sleep was creeping in. She was slowly giving the air a head butt too when she heard a sound and jerked awake.

Like a teenager who was trying so hard to sneak out of the house for a night party, Iman had been tiptoeing through the dark hallway. The lights had gone off, but a ray of light from the dining room refracted across the hallway. She caught Annie's gaze on her.

Iman curiously approached the dining table. Annie buried her head in her face and wiped her eyes carefully, noting all the case files and documents lying on her table. Her laptop was still open, but had hibernated at this time – her tea by the side was only half drunk.

Iman had circled the table now and continued to watch her intently, waiting for the slightest movement.

Annie slowly opened her eyes, her vision was blurry, but when it all came clear and she saw Iman standing there.

"Iman!" she called. She frantically began to gather up the files and documents. "You scared me a little." Then she added with a gentle smile, "Your horror movies are to be blamed."

"I'm sorry," Iman apologized, taking a step backward.

Annie checked the time on her laptop. "It's late. You should be sleeping now," she noted.

Iman hesitated for a while before she spoke. "I couldn't sleep," she said quietly.

The detective paused for a moment and looked at her. "Is everything okay?" she asked.

"I – I had a nightmare."

"Well, those kinds of movies you like to watch are probably the reason. I think it's high time you…" she began, shifting her weight to the right position for a lecture.

"I saw a big, scary looking man with a knife," Iman cut in.

Annie swallowed hard. She knew what that meant and where Iman was going with it. She looked into her eyes – the message was becoming clearer.

"There was a lady, too. They were fighting. He didn't want the baby, but she did, so he stabbed her in the tummy and squeezed her neck. I don't think he wanted to, because after, he cried. A lot," Iman revealed.

Annie let her eyes flutter rapidly like the wings of a butterfly. This was a huge revelation – one she thought Iman had been holding back all this while.

"Then what happened?" she inquired.

"I ran."

Iman kept her eyes at Annie, not looking away for a moment. Annie saw the fear in them, but she wanted her to let them all first. "Did you see his face, Iman?" she said quietly.

Her chest heaved steadily when Iman nodded.

"I only went back to see if it was real," she added.

"It's okay," Annie said. She stretched forward and rubbed down on her shoulders. Iman fought back the tears – her face had gone crimson.

"But she was dead," she concluded.

And the tears betrayed her efforts. Just like in the wheel, they flowed freely. She gasped and sobbed. Annie pulled her into her embrace and wrapped her arms around her same way a mother would do.

CHAPTER SEVENTEEN

The sun shined differently upon Naif Police Station as if it too knew a light was going to shine on some secrets today. The sun rays traveled across the sky, beating down on the roof of the station and casting shadows all around. A couple of eager journalists were setting up for the day like vultures scouring a dead beast. Almost as if they too knew something was going to happen.

Annie still didn't know when her heart beat uncomfortably. She and Iman were in the observation room. Robert Bloom was behind the one-way mirror. He was sitting alone, nervous. Iman was to identify if he was the one she had seen that night of the murder.

Iman took a careful look at Bloom. But after a few seconds, she turned to the detective and shook her head.

Detective Fakir let out a troubled sigh. She knew that *that* automatically set Bloom free. Now she would have to start all over again to look for this suspect that Iman would easily identify. She had really put her hope that the killer was definitely Bloom. But now she had to let him go. She nodded stiffly at an officer nearby who then left them.

There were a few more members of the press outside the station now. There was indistinct chattering amongst them as they waited for the latest developments.

Soon enough, the station's doors opened and Robert Bloom walked through, accompanied by his lawyer. There was now a stampede amongst the members of the press. Bloom and his lawyer made their way down the stairs, squeezing past the Journalists who jostled and crowded around them.

Mister Bloom, will you say a few words?

How does it feel to be out of there?

What do you say to the people who accused you of this?

That last question was the charm. Bloom and his lawyer stopped.

"I can't say anything about the case, but I will say that my client is one hundred percent innocent and looking forward to getting back to his life. Now, if you'll please…" he declared, causing Annie to clench her teeth from behind the window she watched. The lawyer led Bloom through the crowd. They were followed the same way fans of a celebrity would do.

What does this mean for the rest of the investigation?

Is Annie Fakir competent enough to solve this case?

The journalists continued to throw more and more questions at Bloom and his lawyer, but neither of them gave a response. They finally got to where the lawyer had parked his car, got in and drove away, leaving the journalists with their insatiable appetite for answers.

Annie sighed and turned away. She had been called into the office of the head of the department and she suspected similar answers would be thrown her way. She braced herself.

***

Annie and Iman sat on a bench overlooking the Persian Gulf. It was blustery and the waves howled pitilessly. The wind blew over the sea, carrying sweet-smelling mists up in the air. Their hair gave whooshing sounds as they flew backwards and some across their faces. Iman was not wearing her beanie today. She explained to Annie already that she wanted to let in some air down her scalp. She too must have had a lot to think about. Annie knew the girl's breakdown the other night had taken quite a toll. She understood that.

On the other hand, Annie had her mind emptied and blank right now. She didn't want to think about the case or the pressure it brought upon her head. She'd even switched off her phone just for whatever few minutes of peace she could grasp.

Sitting across the bench next to them was a woman Annie thought was pretty nosey. She would probably be in her 60s. Annie had spotted her taking a picture of her with her phone. And when she noticed that she had been caught, she quickly hid the phone. And now, Annie was no longer comfortable here – she wanted to leave. So much for peace.

"Do you wanna eat out tonight?" she asked Iman.

Iman looked at her, not particularly excited about the question that sounded more like an offer. "Where?" she asked.

"Anywhere you want," Annie answered.

Iman smiled and her eyes seem to brighten with a thought almost instantly. Annie continued to glance at the woman till it was time to leave and Iman told her where she would like them to be.

***

Erol's restaurant wasn't quite empty this night. Iman noticed the chubby girl form the other day who asked an awful lot of questions, and a younger man sitting on stools directly before the counter. Then there was Iman and An-nie. They were each halfway through a mighty kebab. Erol, on the other hand, was cleaning the back of the counter as he and his friends spoke gently. The TV played at the back-ground with no one really paying attention to it.

Annie took a huge bite and got hot sauce all over her cheeks. Iman chuckled. "What?" the detective asked.

Iman pointed to her cheeks.

"Hey, it isn't a real kebab if you don't get it all over your face," Annie said, a smile hovered around her lips. She wiped herself with the napkin curtly.

"When I was a student in England, I lived off of these things," she added. "They were never spicy enough though. White people can't handle the spices. Don't tell Eliza I said that."

"You like it spicy?" Iman asked, wearing a cheeky smile.

Annie all but scoffed in unbridled surprise. "You don't?"

"I never tried it," said Iman. In fact this restaurant was the first place she ever tried kebab in her life. It was mostly sweets and baked food when it came to her mother.

"Here!" Annie grabbed a bottle of hot sauce and squeezed some onto the edge of Iman's plate. "Go on, try it," she told her.

Iman carefully dipped her kebab in the sauce and took a bite. "Hmm…"

"Good, right?" Annie asked with a light smile.

Iman nodded.

Annie took another bite of the kebab. She munched on it till there was little of it left in her mouth and then she said, "You were brave today. It took a lot to do what you did. You realize that, right?

"But it wasn't him," Iman said – she sounded a bit modest. "I know, but still…"

Iman coughed. The heat of the sauce had burnt her

throat. Annie laughed as she took a napkin and handed it to Iman.

"You'll get used to it, trust me," she added.

As Iman wiped her nose, Annie was drawn to the TV behind her and Iman's gaze followed. A report was going on outside the police station, clearly shot earlier today. Iman didn't recognize the woman reported the news.

"Despite being released from police custody this morning, Creek Municipality has officially dropped Robert Bloom as a partner in its developments for a new five-star beach front hotel. The project was the cause of much debate among residents prior to the murder of Yasmin Hojat…" she said curtly. The scene switched to another woman who continued with the news in Arabic.

Annie caught eyes with Erol. "You'll get him," he assured. Annie smiled and Erol went back to what he was doing.

One of his friends, Janet, was saying, "The daughter apparently married some nobody from Europe and he could just inherit the whole of Creek Observer Inc." Erol and the other man were quick to share their thoughts on whoever Janet spoke about.

Iman smiled gently. She liked Erol and the way he accepted the news when Iman and Annie showed up earlier. The both of them had acquainted themselves and talked a bit about Iman. Annie had carefully left out Iman's involvement in the case, which the girl appreciated. And her heart warmed now that she saw the kebab seller easily chatting with friends.

"Eliza doesn't like it spicy? Is Eliza still with you?" Iman questioned. If Annie thought Iman hadn't put the pieces of their relationship together, she was wrong. Iman clearly knew that such practice was not cherished in the town and as such she had asked the question in a whisper. The whole idea wasn't strange to her though.

Annie looked at her briefly and then at Erol. He was still busy chatting with his friends, and that told them that he had not heard a word of that. "I hope so. Why do you ask?" she intoned.

Iman shrugged, feigning disinterest. She put more hot sauce onto her plate.

Annie watched, but her mind was no longer here, Iman noticed. Several thoughts had occupied her mind and Iman knew Eliza was carefully nestled in one of those thoughts.

***

Night came just like the day. Annie sat on the couch with her phone. After a moment's hesitation, she began to type.

"I'm sorry..."

After she had clicked on send, she threw her phone on the couch and brought the TV to life with the remote, while watching her phone with the corner of her eye for a response.

In no time, she heard the doorbell ring. She looked at her phone, but there was no message. She wondered who it was at the door. But she reached for it. Through the peephole, she saw that it was Eliza. Her heart leapt.

She sheepishly opened the door to Eliza, who had a wry grin on her face. Eliza walked in. She dropped her bag on the floor and kissed Annie, who couldn't help but laughed. And then she shut the door behind her. Or, at least, that was what she was going to do. But Annie noticed a folder at one corner of her building.

"What's that?" she asked.

Eliza raised a brow. "I didn't even take note of it when I came in," she said cautiously. "Should you be doing that?"

Annie picked up the folder despite her girlfriend's protest. She was careful while handling the thin brown folder. It clearly wasn't a bomb, so she wasn't that cautious. However, she held it at the very edge, trying not to get her prints all over it. Though a part of her told her the folder was clean of any other fingerprint.

"Be careful," Eliza told her.

"Always." Annie gave her an encouraging smile. They both remained at the doorway as Annie opened the folder and gently pulled out its content.

It was a picture, it appeared. The moment Annie saw it, her gaze snapped up and she scanned the immediate surroundings of their quiet neighborhood. Then she and Eliza sank into the house quickly.

"Is that…"

Annie nodded. "Yes. It's me and you… kissing." This picture certainly wasn't the one the reporter had taken the other day. In this picture, Eliza and Annie had been in the house. Annie could feel her heart pounding within the confinement of her ribcage but she still managed to ease her breath as she turned the picture around.

There, written in blood red ink, and in bold letters were the words, "I SEE YOU. YOU COULD BE NEXT."

Eliza gasped. Annie looked around them, careful to note that Iman wasn't nearby. Then she looked through the peephole of her door. This was clearly a warning form Yasmin Hojat's killer. He knew Annie's secret and he could just use it against her. The message was clear. He was telling her to stay off his case.

But that also meant Annie was closer. She just wasn't sure how much she would be risking by finding the murderer.

***

The Man could sniff out a problem from a mile away, like a blood hound. And that was why he tried to cut it down at its root before it hurt him. Yasmin Hojat had been a problem, and Annie Fakir was now a problem too.

He just had to make sure she left the case so he could tie it all up nicely and live his life.

CHAPTER EIGHTEEN

Detective Annie Fakir swallowed down her fear. The message from the previous night still drifted about in her vision, and along it this tightening in her chest. Regardless, she had been quick to get dressed and come for an interview she'd been forced to attend. A quick glance at the time revealed it was 14:21pm. A little distance from where Annie's mind had been trying to figure out the best way to react to the murderer's message, Dylan Smith was there. He was standing by the beach front – the crab box storage area was cordoned off with the 'crime zone' tape behind him. It was raining and so he held an umbrella.

Standing nearby was a group of protesters with signs that read: "FAKIR OUT", "BANG UP BLOOM", "JUSTICE FOR YASMIN". Annie was aware of the all the messages and protests that went on the internet and various social medias, but seeing the people of Deira in this form of bold protest made her uncomfortable.

Her gaze moved on to her interviewer for the afternoon. He was dressed as smartly as he was the last time he'd interviewed her. Annie already believed Dylan was the poster child for all Creek Observer interviews. Now she had to hope he wouldn't throw her under the bus again. Even though she knew it was a fat chance.

"You'll be fine, detective," Officer Kazeem said behind Annie underneath the tent that'd been set up for the interview. Annie nodded. She was yet to tell him, or anyone, of the threat. And she wouldn't be able to tell them because of what she risked revealing.

Instead she cleared her throat and sat on the chair as Dylan came to his too. The rain kept pouring around them when the camera began rolling.

"The pressure is building for Deira Police today as the residences demand answers regarding the seaside murder. I'm here live with Detective Annie Fakir, the detective in charge of the case," announced Dylan, wearing a curt smile.

Annie tried her best to mirror a smile close enough with that.

"Good afternoon, Detective Fakir. Thank you for being here in this dreadful weather. I know it's a busy time."

"My pleasure, Dylan," Annie replied.

The European man nodded and straightened in his seat. "It seems like it is one step forward and two steps backward for you right now, don't you think? I can only imagine how frustrated you must feel," he said, a hint of pity in his voice.

"Well, we may have acted slightly too fast in…"

"The murder weapon was missing from a set of knives in Robert Bloom's kitchen," Dylan cut in. "How do you let your prime suspect walk away like that?"

Annie smiled tightly. "There were simply no grounds to hold him," she revealed what she was sure many people already knew.

"Does that mean you'll continue to treat mister Bloom as a suspect?"

"I'm not at liberty to say, but I will conform that we do have a lead in the case," said Annie. The interview continued in the same back and forth without Annie revealing too much. There was no way she would let people know about Iman. Who knew what threat could rest on the poor girl's head? That was also the reason Annie had allowed Iman spend the afternoon someplace safe while she dealt with this.

Even then, her gaze kept travelling through the crowd.

I SEE YOU. YOU COULD BE NEXT.

***

"Hey, Iman. Look, it's your friend," Erol announced, pointing at the TV. His tone flattened when he muttered, "And Fatima too." Iman lifted her gaze to see Annie on the screen for a while. "She looks scared," she commented. Though Iman was unaware of probably a lot of details, she knew there was a reason Annie had dropped her off here at Erol's instead of just leaving her at home like she'd done the previous day.

"What? *Laa*," he said. *No.* The man gestured for the TV. "She's doing fine... You know, I might have to close this place down soon too."

"You will?" Iman's gaze lit up in surprise. Not in a million years would she have thought that he would even think of that. She looked around the place. There had been a time she had called it home, no matter how little. It was her source of life when she had nowhere to eat from. How could he say that?

Erol shrugged and leaned against a side of the counter as the interview kept playing in the background. "Mm-hmm."

"That's sad," Iman commented, concealing her actual emotions.

"But I don't know. It'll give me chance to finish my projects. I've got houses all over that are just sat there in ruins..." he explained further. "Maybe I will open it sometime again. Maybe."

Iman glanced at the TV to see how Annie was doing, but her focus glued when he caught sight of something. Someone.

They were talking about some rumors surrounding Annie now, and the detective was explaining how rumors weren't the best things for one to pay attention to at a time like this.

"I think I'll start with Chapel Park," Erol continued. "I put some money away last year for..."

As Erol babbled away, Iman kept her gaze on the TV,

paying no attention to what Erol was saying. Her mouth fell slightly open.

Erol's voice was suddenly engulfed by a high-pitched sound. Everything appeared to spin and go in slow motion. Iman focused on a particular set of eyes on the screen. There was Annie there, the interviewer and a particular officer who was vaguely familiar to Iman. She panted for breath, wobbled her feet and squinting her eyes. It was like a terrible migraine. She had to shut her eyes contain the riot going in her head.

But when she opened them, her surroundings were blurry. She heard Erol's voice calling her – it sounded distant, as though she were underwater.

Iman inhaled deeply and shut her eyes again. When she opened them the second time, everything came to focus.

"Everything all right?" Erol asked, panic in his voice and a hint of fear in his eyes.

Iman turned her gaze at him, mirroring the same panic in Erol's eyes, then bolted out the restaurant, the door jiggling behind her. Erol called out her name behind her but she didn't pause. Her feet led her to the place it had all began.

Most people said murderers returned to the scene of a crime, but Iman wouldn't have guessed just how close to the scene this one was. Those eyes came flashing through her mind over and over again. Iman felt like she was back in that construction site, hiding within the embrace of the darkness as the man searched for her. And she saw him.

Iman whizzed down the street, panting in desperation. The rain showed no pity as she cut across the drops in her path. She had to warn Annie.

****

As if Annie wasn't getting irritable enough, Dylan led her over to the group of protesters under another tent. They both held their umbrellas as they walked through the wet ground.

"Good afternoon, everyone," Dylan greeted and then added in a wonky Arabic accent, "*Masa' ul-hayr*." The crowd muttered mixed responses to the greeting. "I'm Dylan Smith from Creek Observer Online. Is there anything you'd like to say to Detective Fakir?"

A brunette woman Annie recognized from an earlier interview spoke up. "What are the chances the killer could strike again? We are living in fear each and every day," she said.

"There's no need to live in fear. I am certainly not. We're confident this wasn't a random attack. The killer knew the victim. He had a reason to murder her," Detective Fakir answered.

"The baby?" a fat woman in an abaya said.

Annie nodded. That was one thing they were sure of thought she was yet to see it as enough motivation. "Sadly, yes. That's what we've come to believe," she said.

There was a second of silence.

"Anyone else?" Dylan asked.

An angry-looking old man snatched the microphone from him. He wore a dirty kandora with a turban on his head and a wave of bears around his chin. He seemed like one of the fishermen. "You're a disgrace, Annie Fakir! Lock Bloom back in his cell and throw away the damn key," he snarled as his words dropped with a strong Arabic accent. He turned quickly to the protesters behind him and declared something to them in Arabic.

From somewhere in the group, someone began to chant, "Lock him up. Lock him up."

The rest of the group soon joined in. And in a short while the chants resounded across the walls of the beach and beyond.

Dylan turned to the camera. Annie backed away, unsure what to do with herself. The chants were ringing through her head and she wished it was all over so she could go home and lock herself in a room.

But it wasn't like she could just up and leave in front of live television, so she stood her ground, edged on by an encouraging smile from Kazeem.

"Well, as always, the people of Deira voicing their opinion, and as you can see, emotions are high. They all beckon for justice," said Dylan.

Quite unexpectedly, Iman rushed up behind Annie and nudged her. Detective Fakir turned. She was surprised to see Iman drenched and gulping in mouthfuls of air. Iman gave her a sign to bend over which Annie did by bringing the umbrella closer to the girl. And when she did Iman whispered something in her ear.

Detective Fakir's face quickly assumed a different expression – that of pure savagery. Her gaze observed her surroundings. There, she realized something she'd felt stupid for not realizing sooner. Someone had left footprints in the semiarid ground, and as she inspected them, she wasn't very surprised now to see they had a unique crisscross pattern.

She looked up at Dylan who was now facing the camera and down at his feet. Iman had named Dylan Smith as the murderer of Yasmin Hojat.

"I am Dylan Smith for Creek Observer Online. Thank you for joining us," finished Dylan.

Soon, they were all back at the first tent. While the cameraman packed up his gear, Dylan threw shady glances at Detective Fakir and Iman.

The protesters were still milling around, chatting amongst each other.

Annie was crouched face to face with Iman, her hands on Iman's shoulders. Iman nodded her head vehemently. They both looked over at Dylan who forced a half-hearted smile back at them.

And now the rain was heavier than Dubai might have ever experienced. The windstorm it created was strong enough to rocket a sunshade across the sky. If the Anti-Bloom protesters liked themselves, they should probably pack up and leave.

A deep grey sky loomed over the barren high street. The shops were closed – the people had run to the safety of their homes. A powerful gust of wind sent a plastic bag across the air, swirling it at top speed. The clouds were moving faster, as giving space for a brighter sky. But the rain continued to lash out mercilessly on everything it touched. Peals of thunder rumbled and crashed ruthlessly. It was like the world that revolved around Deira had finally come to an end. Perhaps nature itself wanted justice for Yasmin as well.

But none of that compared to the fury Annie herself nursed for Dylan Smith.

CHAPTER NINETEEN

In the interrogation room came the moment of truth. Just like before, Detective Fakir watched Dylan through the one-way mirror. Dylan was alone in the room, staring at the door as if he had not seen a thing like that before. On the table was a bottle of water. After the whispering by Iman, Detective Fakir had wasted no time in bringing him in. And for that to have happened, she was sure he knew something was amiss.

Annie finally entered the room with Officer Kazeem at her side. Dylan drank from the bottle next to him. Looking closely at him, one could tell that he was only trying to build up courage.

"Sorry to keep you waiting. Thanks for coming in," Annie said as she walked to the chair opposite him. She kept the recorder she had come with on the table.

Dylan looked at it and then up at her. He knew what it was and what it could do if he spoke unreasonably. After all, he was a reporter too. "I am a busy man, Annie. What's this all about?" he intoned.

Annie shuffled on the chair. "Actually, we've made some progress on the case," she said. Her voice was reeked of confidence this time.

"That's great," Dylan remarked.

"Yeah, it is."

Dylan laughed nervously. "Do you want to tell me what it is so I can report it at Creek Observer, or...?" he trailed on.

"A witness came forward."

"Oh wow! A witness?" His face creased like he wasn't sure he heard that right.

"Yeah," Annie confirmed with a light smile, giving him that I-got-you kind of look.

"Hmm…"

Annie decided it was time to quit stalling and get down to business. It was time to get serious. She glared at Dylan. He must have considered her glare as a joke because he began to chuckle ever so lightly. However, the laughter was wiped clean off his face when he observed that the detective was no longer laughing.

"What's going on, Annie?" he questioned.

"Did you ever have any kind of relationship with Yasmin Hojat?" she asked, keeping her voice stern.

Dylan's rumpled as if he had just been asked directly if it was he who killed Yasmin. "No, I never knew the girl," he answered.

"The thing is, this witness says they saw you with her that night of the murder."

"Saw me? Where?" Dylan scoffed.

"At the beach."

"What? No, I…"

Annie placed her hand on the table and leaned forward. "Listen, Dylan, I have a witness willing to testify in a court of law that they saw you murder Yasmin Hojat."

"I… there's no… who?" He fumbled for words, his forehead wrinkling into a frown and straightening over and over again.

The detective shook her head and tapped her fingers on the table.

"That girl you were with at the beach… This is ridiculous, Annie. You're going to listen to a little girl?" he questioned. With the new frown on his face, Annie could tell his mind was drawing p Iman's face from the set of the interview less than an hour ago.

"You made this entire city believe it was Bloom who killed her. You almost had me, too... We found prints, Dylan," revealed Annie.

Dylan shook his head, shifting his gaze between Annie

and Officer Kazeem. "There were no fingerprints. You told me that yourself," he said.

"Not fingerprints – footprints."

"I don't understand."

"At Fifty-four Chapel Park, crystal clear in the dust were footprints. They were an exact match with your shoes," she explained further, collecting a tablet from Kazeem and turning it to Dylan. "Look familiar?"

Dylan was beginning to sense he was in trouble now. His eyes went in an unfocused gaze. Beads of tears could be seen creeping out of their pores.

"Wait. How did you…"

Annie withdrew the tablet and placed it before her, tapping slowly. "Since your memory is a bit blurry, let me give you a quick rundown of what happened," she said curtly. "You got married to Farah Zarouni last month, didn't you?" She didn't want for a response. "Her father owns Creek Observer too, doesn't he? Given your marriage to Farah, you've managed to land a good job at Creek Observer. Good interviews, by the way. But this also means you get to inherit the entirety of Creek Observer when Mr. Zarouni dies. Think of all the money and the fame and everything… And all of that would be threatened if Yasmin Hojat kept that baby. Maybe Farah would have divorced you and it would be back to rock bottom. Wherever that is."

Annie paused for emphasis. Kazeem had been the one to dig up all the research so she couldn't really take credit for it. The officer had noticed, however, that there was practically no record of Dylan Smith before he married Farah.

"Maybe you thought killing Yasmin was the only way to secure your future. Well, you were wrong." After those words, Dylan struggled to present an answer to Annie. "I think it's best you call your lawyer," she advised.

"You can't just…"Dylan breathes heavily, his palms sweating as even words had begun to fail him. "You're making a mistake!" he warned. "My father-in-law will not stand by and let this--"

"I don't think you understand what's happening, Dylan. It's over. You've been made." Detective Fakir gazed deep in his eyes. It was as though she was already searching for the answers she needed in there.

What had begun as a friendly conversation between two colleagues now turned into a bitter glare.

"I'll send someone by," Annie told him.

And that was the last word. She took the recorder on the table – Dylan seemed to have just newly remembered that something like that was there all the while he was fumbling with the words. She gave him one last pitiful look and then left with Kazeem.

"Annie!" Dylan called, but she was already behind the door. Dylan slammed his fist on the table in frustration – his face had turned scarlet and sweating nervously.

***

In the waiting room, a few residences and offenders sat around. Annie filled up a bottle at the water cooler. Across the room, Dylan was on the station's pay phone. A police officer stood a few yards away from him, keeping watch; Officer Hussain.

Annie peered over at Dylan. He spoke in hushed tones, stealing glances at the officer and slapping his hand against the wall. Officer Hussain's eyes met with those of Detective Fakir's. He cocked his brows and smiled nervously.

"...but I need you!" Dylan blared at the person he was talking with on the other end of the phone. That drew Officer Hussain's focus back to him. He shot a glare at Dylan, who returned to his anxious whispers.

Detective Fakir watched him for a few moments before walking away. She came outside the walls of the station which still had some journalists and reporters waiting around. Annie ignored them as she leaned against the wall and tapped on her phone. Then, she pressed the phone to her ear as it began to ring at the other side.

"Yes. Hi. It's Annie Fakir from Deira Police. I need to speak to someone about a runaway... Sure, I can hold..." she said. Her lips flattened as she considered what she was about to do. It was the right decision to take. She was sure of that. But that night, when Annie would arrived home. Iman would be nowhere to be found. She would search for her throughout the house and realize the young girl was nowhere. Every calls she would make, to Eliza and to Erol would prove fruitless.

Iman was gone.

CHAPTER TWENTY

Night returned. Iman walked along a quiet, dimly lit street, in her big coat and green beanie. It had been a while since she wore her beanie. Now her hair which had firmly received treatments was tucked carefully inside of it. She felt relieved. The killer of Yasmin had finally been arrested. It was like a burden had been taken off her young shoulders. The time she wanted to take to catch her breath in the course of looking for her mother had ended. She was starting to think it was time she resumed the search.

Down the road, she saw a woman in heels cross the road – it was like Yasmin when she went up her house. She stopped and watched her until she disappeared into the darkness of the adjacent street.

Iman followed. She used the night as a cover and kept her gaze on the woman, making sure not to lose track of her. Even when she walked past Erol's restaurant and was tempted to stop for some kebab, she didn't. This was more important.

Iman made no effort to stop and give a second thought to what she was doing. She just strolled along rather impulsively. Until finally, the woman flagged down a taxi got in – she had no idea that someone had been on her trails all the while. Iman was left alone at the blustery shore front. That was when he gave up. Still, her feet refused to take her back home to Annie.

So Iman went closer to the beach – the tides had risen and fallen and had now reached her toes. To her right, the lights of the fairground flickered and a beam silhouetted upon the sky.

Just as she admired the momentary beauty, a hand moved in from nowhere and clamped her mouth. Iman tried to fight free. She tried to scream, but it was muffled behind the hand. She was persistently dragged down the shadows of the beach.

A male figure dragged Iman across the construction yard towards the caravan. She squirmed in his grasp, but she was no match for the hand that held her. His face was hidden behind a scarf. It had been a pre-planned attack.

Trudging through the thick mud, the man lost his balance and slipped. Iman seized the opportunity immediately and broke free from his grip. Now she sprinted towards a big metal gate at the end of the yard.

She frantically jiggled the latch, but it was stiff and rusty. She looked behind her. The man was on his feet again and storming towards her.

"Help! HELP ME!" she called.

But help was far from her.

As she tried to climb the gate, the man grabbed her by the waist.

"NO! GET AWAY! HELP!" she called, whipping her legs. But the man held both legs with his wide hand and carried her back towards the beach.

***

Erol was packing up his shop, mulling over the arrest of Dylan Smith, a frequent customer at his restaurant, when he spotted Iman through the window as she passed. A part of him expected her to come in so he would proceed to call Annie and put her mind to rest on the little girl's whereabouts. But when Iman didn't come in, he knew something was wrong.

Concerned, he checked his watch – it was late; well-past 11pm already. He came out of the restaurant, watching as she walked further down the street.

***

Annie was anxious – but as she did not know where to look for Iman, she resolved her fate to luck. She hoped she would return, or maybe she would somehow learn of her whereabouts. Her phone rang then, cutting through the tense silence. She jumped up from the chair and answered it. There had been no Caller ID, so she was quick to conclude it was neither Eliza nor Erol

"*Ahlan,*" she greeted as she straightened in her chair.

"Is this Annie Fakir?" a soft female voice spoke.

"Yes," Annie answered, hoping it was what she wanted to hear at this time.

"I'm calling to… well… I don't want to waste your time…" the woman said, a strange accent tinting her words.

Annie frowned. "Who is this?" she asked.

"I've been following your case. Yasmin Hojat. I think I may have found something that could be of interest," the woman explained. "I've attached a file and sent it to your mail that'll shed some light on what you're not seeing."

Annie did not say another word. Instead, she rushed to the dining room and opened up her laptop. The phone was still pressed against her ear. She opened the newest mail she found and clicked on the file attacked to it. Her screen was soon plagued by numerous newspaper clippings and they all spoke about one person… Dylan.

Annie scanned through headline after headline.

"Bloom Brothers receive million-dollar contract for bridge in Dubai."

That was the first that struck Annie's heart, especially when she saw the image positioned beneath it. Two men, one older than the other, sitting on their chair. Dylan was far too young in it, and he was blonde too but if one looked past all that, the faces matched.

"Robert Bloom and his brother, Richard Bloom, to face charges for embezzlement."

"Richard Bloom dead in Dubai Creek boat crash."

The next headline carefully left out Richard now. And they all seemed to follow on Robert. But Annie already knew that Richard Bloom was the same person as Dylan Smith.

"He faked his death and returned after few years?" she said in a broken whisper.

A curt answer came from the other end of the line. "Richard... Dylan skipped university to gain hands on experience and quickly became an integral part of his brother's company. After eighteen months as Chief Operating Officer and with the force of Bloom's charges, they both conspired to save him," she explained. "Richard Bloom died and Dylan Smith moved to London to pursue a career in journalism. And now, he's back to take all he feels is owed."

Annie listened to those words as she slipped on her shoes so fast it was a miracle she didn't trip. She was soon out the door too and making her way for her car.

"How do you know all of this? Who are you?" Annie asked the woman.

There was a pause at the other end of the call. "I'm just a concerned citizen." A beep followed. Annie brought the phone to her face and confirmed that the person had hung up.

Quickly, she tapped on her phone and sent a call to Kazeem. The man picked up quickly. His greetings was barely out his tongue when Annie said, "Can you check who

Dylan made a call to earlier today? Help me find out if it's Robert Bloom."

Then she started the car and was driving into the night.

CHAPTER TWENTY-ONE

Robert Bloom was halfway through a bottle of wine when his brother called him. "They finally caught you, didn't they? About time," he sneered into the phone.

"I'm so sorry, brother," came Dylan's composed voice.

"Don't be. I'm not."

Robert was about to hang up when Dylan said quickly, "You have got to help me got out of here. Please." There was a plea in his voice and that told Robert he was out of options. Dylan always planned things, just like he had done with faking his death and Yasmin's murder, and framing Robert for it. But now he was out of options.

A dry chuckle escaped Robert's lips and he dropped the bottle of wine on the floor. "Why should I? You tried to frame me for Yasmin's murder," he said.

There was a moment of silence. "I was a bit angry at you. I blamed you for what happened to us and the construction company. I thought

I would be punishing you by framing you for that. I'm sorry," was Dylan's defeated response.

With a sigh, Robert mulled over those words. He'd known his brother resented him after the whole corruption charges. "Well, it's too late for that. I can't help you."

"But I need you," pleaded Dylan.

At this, Robert frowned deeply. "You do, huh? Well, I was trying to get my life together once again and your little framing has sent me back to the bottom. Why the fuck should I help you?" he spat into the phone.

"Because I can save you," said Dylan. His voice had been schooled into an even tone now. "Together, with my marriage to Farah Zarouni, who's also pregnant, we can forge a new path for ourselves. Think about what we can do with the money, brother. You could finally get out of that dump and start a new life."

Those words sparked something in Robert's mind. He looked around at the place he was currently in. That hotel job had been his last hope. Now that it was gone it seemed he would remain in this dump.

"How am I sure you're not just going to throw me under the bus again?" he asked.

Dylan sighed. "I won't. I promise. I just need you to do one simple thing for me. For the detective, I have something to use against her, but you have to handle the girl," he said.

****

Back at the construction yard, Iman was thrown onto the couch with her hands tied behind her back. She screamed, but the man straddled her, turned her around and sealed her mouth with duct tape.

He stood over her. The hate in their eyes was mutual. It had been Bloom all the while. His cold eyes were unmistakably identifiable. Iman's eyes wild with terror as she panted heavily.

Bloom pulled up a stool and sat close to Iman. She still had the duct tape across her lips and her hands were still tied behind her but her struggle still pressed on.

"Is it true you saw my brother kill that girl?" he asked quietly after a moment.

Iman nodded.

Bloom closed his eyes and wiped his forehead as if it was a truth he didn't want to hear in the first place. He shuffled his stool closer to Iman.

"No. It wasn't him. I don't know who you are or how you got involved in this but you need to get away from here. Bad things will happen if you don't. Really – really bad things, okay? Do you understand?" he explained to her.

Iman nodded

A tiny gleam settled in his eyes at her response. "That means no testifying in court. You need to tell them it wasn't him. You made a mistake. He didn't do this... Can you promise me?" he asked softly like someone who was out of hope and was now simply clinging to crumbs. Iman hesitated. She knew there was no way she would get out of here and find her mother if she didn't. So she nodded.

Bloom glared at her for a while and then he took a deep breath. He stood up and headed towards the kitchen. He grabbed a bottle of whiskey – his hands shook fervidly. Even in his state, it was time to celebrate. He lowered the scarf and took a swig of the drink.

Suddenly, a sound alerted the both of them, and soon, Bloom was storming towards the window. He peeked through the closed blinds. Iman tried to see. She was turned towards the window like Bloom was. And there was Annie across the yard, by the gate.

And as Annie swung the gate open, she spotted Bloom at the window the same time he spotter her and ducked behind a rusty burn barrel.

With a grunt, Bloom took some moment to reach for a nearby switch. Suddenly, the lights in the caravan went out. Iman watched the man return. Bloom continued to look out through the blinds under the cover of darkness.

Iman mumbled, but Bloom made the sibilant sign of whispering. Iman felt silent at once, and she did the only thing she could do. She watched.

"Bloom! It's me, Annie. No one else is here. Is she safe?" the detective's voice echoed from across the yard.

Bloom cracked open the window. "She's safe," Bloom confirmed.

Drawing confidence from Bloom's response, Annie walked out from behind the burn barrel and approached the caravan. "Why are you doing this?" she questioned.

"Don't come any closer!" Bloom warned.

Annie stopped in her tracks. "Talk to me," she said.

"I don't really have a choice. This is my only way to save my life," he answered. But Bloom could not say another word – he broke down in a whimper. Iman felt a touch of his hopelessness again as she watched him. He was like her in a way, searching for something lost and probably wouldn't be found. "You're a fool, Robert. What were you thinking?" he cursed amidst his sobs.

Iman watched from the couch in silence, her heart still racing like sheet lightening. She watched Annie draw closer as Bloom was distracted by his sobbing.

"I was never going to hurt her, I swear," he confessed. He looked at Iman who was still in the chair and then all around where he lived. He let out a final sigh before his eyes fell upon the door. And there went the silence, before the strike of action.

Suddenly, the door to the caravan flew open and Bloom stormed out. Iman was a bit startled by his action. Then she watched Annie gave a chase, but Bloom sprinted over to a pile of pallets. Swiftly, he climbed onto a storage shed and jumped out of the confines of the yard.

Annie slowed down and cussed a little bit. She turned her attention to the caravan and began to race towards Iman. Annie entered the caravan and found Iman tied up and bound to the couch.

"My goodness!" she exclaimed. She rushed over, peeled off the duct tape and untied her hands.

Iman gasped for breath. Annie moved the sweaty strands of hair that had stuck out of her beanie out of her face and stroked her cheek.

"It's okay. You're safe. I'm here now," she assured.

Annie hugged Iman and kissed her on the forehead. It was like Iman had finally found the mother she was looking for.

***

Bloom bolted along a dark lane, away from the construction site. But someone jumped and tackled him to the ground. It was Erol. He'd been standing by Annie's car where she'd parked it a distance away from the yard. She'd instructed him to only show his face after Annie confirmed Iman was secure. But seeing bloom, he had no reason to strike.

They fell into a heap of dirt. Bloom struggled, but Erol forced himself on top. And with a well-aimed punch to the jaw, he dropped to the ground and faded.

Erol whipped his hand in pain, panting heavily.

Erol Bilginer was not supposed to be here, but he was starting to feel otherwise.

CHAPTER TWENTY-TWO

Gohar was more connected to the case than she had told the detective when she called the other night. She sat in the middle of an almost-empty restaurant, eating kebab while she watched the news on the TV with the restaurant owner.

"THE BLOOM TAPES LEAKED – DAMNING EVIDENCE OF BROTHERS IN CRISIS," read the headline underneath the reporter on the TV. A mugshot of Dylan – no, Richard Bloom – had the caption was positioned at one corner of the screen too.

"Former reporter for the Creek Observer Online, Dylan Smith, and ex-husband of Farah Zarouni has been charged with the murder of sex worker Yasmin Hojat," the reporter continued to explain. "The investigation had also proved Dylan Smith is, in fact, Richard Bloom, a man once thought dead."

Down the screen a new photograph of Robert Bloom in handcuffs popped-up. He was looking dirty, worn out and walking down the lane, escorted by two officers escorting him.

The reporter continued, "After a heroic residence's arrest, the suspect's brother, Robert Bloom, faces charges for evading arrest, kidnapping and accessory to murder…"

Gohar smiled carefully at the news. She was a breed carefully made. She had jet black hair that flowed down her back like water down an undulating hill. Her big wide eyes were sharp like those of a cat and were a very mesmerizing shade of brown. It was as though they could see through one's soul. She had warm bronze skin that gleamed when the sun touched it.

She stared intently at the faces of the men who had driven her husband's firm into bankruptcy and had also led to his suicide later on. She sighed deeply.

"Rest in peace, Farid," the woman said as she turned away.

Just when she was about to resume eating her kebab, a FACETIME call popped on the screen of the laptop before her. The computer's camera automatically turned on. She answered the call. It was from a social worker she'd been working closely with; Rachel.

"Hey," she greeted.

The woman who popped on the screen had a green veil around her hair and her face was heavily made, not to mention all the jewelry she was wearing. "Hey, So, I have some news. Are you sitting down?" Rachel asked.

"I am," she intoned.

"I just got off the phone with Deira Police. They have

Iman. She's here in Dubai. She came to find you, Gohar," she revealed.

A wave of joy and relief washed over the woman at the news, he felt her eyes water instantly. "Is she safe?" Gohar inquired.

"She's safe, but she's been through a lot. There are some things you need to know. It is better coming from me before the press gets a hold of it. Can we meet?"

"I'm free right now," Gohar answered.

"My office, one hour?"

"I'll be there."

"See you then."

"Bye."

Gohar Mehrabi got up almost quickly, abandoning the kebab. She limped out the door of the restaurant with her laptop in hand. Her mind flashed over to the last time she'd seen her daughter.

It was that afternoon in the train. Their train had been attacked by some people who rigged the railway. She re-membered the last touch of Iman she felt before her daughter fell through the window. Gohar and many others had been with those bandits for quite some time, and the first thing she had done when she got out was to find her daughter.

It's been over a year and her best lead had been a dead

woman named Angie. Gohar had arrived in Deira after giving up all hope. And now, her search had come to an end.

***

Annie and Iman sat on the couch in the living room.

Eliza looked out the window. "Still nothing," she commented.

"You're stressing me out," Annie replied. "They're ten minutes late. They probably hit traffic." She turned to Iman, noticing the glum look on her face. "You okay?"

Iman nodded. But Annie noticed her picking her nails. She didn't want to go. But she knew at the same time that she didn't have much of a choice. She could only make a face.

When Eliza came down to the couch, she muttered to Annie, "Are you sure Dylan can't just out you with that picture?"

"Kazeem helped gather all the copies in his house while the police searched there. Thankfully, he didn't show anyone except me," she answered, keeping her voice quiet too. "Hopefully, there isn't more. But it's bound to come one of these days anyway." Eliza gave her hand a squeeze. Then Annie lifted her gaze and said, "That's why I told my parents already."

Eliza blinked. "What? Why? What did they say?" she demanded.

"Nothing. My brother is cool with it though. I'm sure my parents will come around eventually," she answered. If Iman hadn't been there, Annie would have just taken Eliza in her arms and kissed her stupidly. But she resisted the urge. Instead, the both of them kept holding hands as Eliza kept looking out the window.

"Wait. There's a car. I think it's them," Eliza announced finally, rising to her feet.

Annie and Eliza came through the door to meet the people they expected. There was the social worker, Rachel, and Iman's mother Gohar Mehrabi who was holding hands with a handsome Persian man. They exchanged pleasantries and introduced themselves. The man introduced himself as Jamshid. Annie then gestured them inside.

"Hi, Iman," Rachel greeted. She was the first to come through.

"Hi," Iman responded lethargically.

"It's nice to see you again," she added.

And just then, Iman looked up and saw her mother, Gohar sashaying into the living room.

"Look at you. You're so big. So pretty," Gohar crooned – a tear dropped off her eyes. She was smiling at the same time and wiping the tears off her eyes.

Iman could not believe her eyes. It was her mother. She was willing to travel to the ends of the world just so she could see her again. Her heart was pumping harder now. And with joy beyond her control, Iman strode swiftly across the room and wrapped her hands around her mother, squeezing tightly. Gohar could not contain herself. The tears flowed like an endless river. She fell on her knees, stroking her daughter's face. Perhaps not as passionate, but she had also been looking for her. The emotions were the same as a blind mother that had just found her only child.

"I'm so sorry, Iman," she cried.

"I found you," Iman responded.

"You did. You really did."

Gohar stroked Iman's hair and stood up. Annie handed her a box of tissues and she took some, blowing her nose.

"I'm sorry," she excused herself.

"Please, have a seat," Annie gestured.

"I'll make some tea," Eliza volunteered and headed into the kitchen.

Annie sat with Iman. Gohar, Jamshid and Rachel squeezed into the other couch.

"So, here we are," Rachel noted.

"I can't thank you enough for everything you've done. Truly, it's difficult to put into words," Gohar said to Annie.

"Well, if it wasn't for your call, who knows where we would be?" Annie replied. They'd made acquaintances earlier and Gohar had explained further how Iman's father, Farid Mehrabi, was connected with the Bloom Brothers, and the woman had only stumbled upon the case while watching TV one day. She'd made sure to expose Dylan Smith as Richard Bloom at that point. But who would have thought how thickly knitted the entire thing truly was?

"Your father and the Blooms were quite tight back in the days." She glanced at Iman and then continued. "I'd done business with both of them. Seeing Richard on TV and realizing he was alive made me try to uncover them."

"Dylan changed his name after the first arrest," Annie said.

"Makes sense! He was always so desperate to be on TV. It was all an act. He was never really like that, you know," said Gohar, sighing. "And think about his wife. I hear she's pregnant."

Annie nodded.

"We've all heard about what you went through, Iman. I can't even imagine how scary it must've been," Rachel threw in.

"She's a brave girl," Annie remarked.

Gohar couldn't take her eyes off Iman. She clutched Jamshid's hand for a proper introduction. "This is Jamshid. He's helped me a lot over the past few years. We're engaged," Gohar said.

"It's nice to finally meet you, Iman," Jamshid greeted with a smile. Annie couldn't help but notice how handsome he was, earning her a blow at her side from Eliza. She chuckled.

Iman, on the other hand, quickly scanned Jamshid up and down. Though, Annie noticed, her interest was short-lived. She seemed to be more concerned with being with her mother.

"We just moved into a farmhouse – to Al Ain. I think you'd like it there," Gohar said.

"Do you think you might want to visit sometime?" Rachel asked.

Iman nodded.

"We'd love to have you," Gohar chipped.

Iman returned to fiddling with her fingers. "Can I stay here?" she asked.

"I'm afraid not," Rachel answered.

"But you can come and stay over for movie night, though. Any time you like," Annie said.

"I'll miss you," Iman crooned.

"I'll miss you too, darling," Annie replied.

After their time at Annie's living room, it was time to go. Iman sat in the front passenger seat, looking out the window at Annie and Eliza, who were standing by the doorway. She and Annie waved each other goodbyes.

Rachel entered the car and strapped on her seat belt.

"Ready to go?" she asked.

The engine revved. Rachel looked back at Gohar and Jamshid in their car. They had wound down their glasses already for the final goodbyes.

"I guess this is goodbye – for now, of course," she intoned.

"Thank you so much, again, for everything," Gohar replied.

"You're welcome. I'll be in touch, okay," she said.

"We'll see you in a couple of weeks, Iman," Gohar promised.

Iman smiled over at her mother. They wound up their windows are drove off. And as they passed the house, Iman took one final look at Annie and Eliza.

Whatever came from their union, she would find out some other time. She would always visit this house she called a home. They cared for her when she longed for the love of a mother. She was grateful to them all. She was grateful to Erol. Someday, she would pay him a visit – to officially thank him for all that he did for her. His restaurant was her source of strength.

But now, she was leaving – leaving to be with her mother. She was reminded of her own words: "I found you". Indeed, she found her. A bitter experience it was, but indeed, she found her.

She was not in any way scared of testifying against Dylan Bloom in court. She would boldly march forward and tell the jury what she saw.

And now, she sat by in the car, looking out the window and reminiscing how it all began.

"I found you," she muttered.

She said the words again and again. But she soon lost to silence, then to sleep.

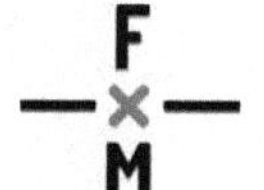